The Last Stand of the Dragon

The Last Stand of the Dragon

N. J. Hanson

Ink Drop Press
Chico, CA

ISBN 13: 978-1-947583-04-7
ISBN 10: 1-947583-04-2

Printed in the United States of America

To Virginia Partain
and Sherry Long

Prologue

A mountain jutted up from the earth. It reached thousands of feet into the air, its time eroded but still mighty jagged peaks pierced the underside of the clouds. Pine trees grew along the mighty granite slopes, their branches covered in a fine powder of freshly fallen snow. Hidden amongst these trees was a cave, a cavern which yawned open like the mouth of an enormous beast and stretched back hundreds of feet into the heart of the mountain.

Inside this cave, hidden in inky blackness and secluded from the rest of he world, was a creature of great size and strength with powers that legends were spoken off. An animal the likes of which had not been seen on this earth for millions of years. Now, the beast slept. Her legs pulled in close against her body and her tail wrapped up to her nose, her chest rose and fell with each breath.

A sound echoed through the cave. The sound of a large boulder being pushed and rolled aside. It was followed by the sound of the rock crashing down the mountainside, causing a miniature land-slide. The creature's eyes fluttered, then snapped fully open. The yellow-green orbs jerked around furiously in their sockets as they adjusted to the darkness. Her slumber had been disturbed.

A new sound reached her ears, rocks being crunched beneath feet and the clink of metal against metal. Voices as well, at least three distinctive voices were heard as they echoed off the walls of her cave.

"You say this is the cave?" The first voice said.

"Ssh." Another responded. "We don't want to awaken it."

Humans. They had come for her yet again. She pushed herself up from the ground, her leg muscles stretched and tensed. With her feet planted firmly on the ground, she flexed open her wings and beat them to work out the stiffness. She stretched out her legs, popped her neck from one side and then the other. As she awoke, her front claws caught on a rib bone which lay on the floor and knocked it away.

Bones lay scattered across the cave floor all around her, animal bones which belonged to the livestock of the nearby village. Sheep bones, pigs, goats, and even the bones of young calves. This was why the humans had come after her again, to put an end to her thieving.

But she had no choice. She must feed herself after all, and food in these mountains had grown incredibly scarce.

The footsteps and voices grew steadily closer. Soon, she knew, they would be upon her and then she would have little means of escape. Humans were physically weak, but also cunning. She would need to draw first blood if she was to escape with her life. She crouched low to the ground and slinked though the cave like a large cat towards the sounds of the intruders.

Ahead of her was a crevice in the wall of her cave, a crack in the rock which reached from the floor all the way to the ceiling, and just big enough at its widest point for her to squeeze in her massive shoulders. With her wings folded tight against her body, she stepped into the crevice backwards with her tail pulled up underneath her. She hugged at the ground, the muscles in her back legs coiled and tense as she waited.

"Rennec," the voice from before echoed, "bring me the torch. And hand me my crossbow."

"Yes, sir." A second, much younger voice, replied.

A flickering light danced along the cave wall. She saw them through the crevice gap as they approached.

The first was a tall man, nearly six feet in height with black hair which reached to his shoulders, and a short beard that grew down from his cheeks to his chin. Upon his face she noted another feature; a large, crescent-shaped scar which started just above his eye and reached all the way down his face to end at his chin. No hair grew over this scar.

His upper body was armored, it glistened and reflected the light from the torch which he held in his right hand. A cape of heavy blue fabric hung from his shoulders and fell all the way down to his feet. Armor plates also adorned his legs over top brown trousers. He held a sword at his waist which still rested in its scabbard.

In his left hand he held a weapon, one unlike any she had seen before. The man gripped the stock like a sword, but it had a small bow and arrow in place of a blade. She did not like that weapon. Bows and arrows had already caused her pain in the past, to see one combined with a sword frightened her.

Another human came up behind the first, this one much younger and significantly smaller. He was dressed in armor much like the first, and drug behind him a sled weighted down with more assorted weapons; from axes to daggers to swords. His hair was short and wavy red, and his face pale and dotted with freckles. "Master Vince," the boy whispered, "is it here?"

"If our guide be true." The taller man, Vince, motioned with the torch to the third man.

The first two humans walked passed the crevice without noticing her, the shadows covered her too well. A third human, the guide who had led them here, came up behind them with his sword already drawn and clutched in his hands. "I swear," he said in a wobbly voice, "this is the cave. This is were that beast lives."

"Well," Vince kicked a rib bone and sent it skidding across the floor. "With all these bone around, it's obvious something very big and carnivorous lives in this cave." He handed the torch back to his assistant, grabbed a lever on the bottom of his weapon, and flexed it forward. A hook caught the bowstring and locked it in place. A bolt shifted from the chamber on the bottom into the smooth channel of the barrel. With that done, he took the torch back from the younger boy. "Come on, but more quietly. With any luck, the creature still sleeps."

The first two humans moved on. They stepped deeper and deeper into the cave, the light from their flame grew dimmer. The guide crept along behind them, his eyes gazed around in fear at every dancing shadow. The creature watched him eagerly from her hiding place.

Her leg muscles tensed up in preparation. Her claws scratched at the ground before her as she waited. The human needed to just take a few more steps and he would be in range. Just a little bit more. He stepped closer, and closer. The guide stopped and his eyes fixed on the crevice in the wall. He stared intently at her, and she stared back. What was he waiting for? Could he see her? If so, why had he not alerted his comrades yet? He just needed to take one more step. Just one more.

The man looked away from her and towards the other humans as they moved away. "Wait for me!" He called. He started to run towards them, and that's when she made her move.

In that instant, the reptile thrust herself out of the crevice. With claws outstretched and mouth agape, she collided with the man. Together they crashed into the far wall, his bones snapped under her enormous weight. Her claws tore at his chest and ripped the armor away as if it were made of paper, and her teeth shredded his neck. The man did not have time to scream before he died. She took the body in her mouth and shook it violently, vertebrae snapped in her jaws and blood flowed down her throat.

"Master, the dragon!" Rennec, the young red-haired child, shouted in alarm.

"I see it!" Vince lifted his crossbow up to eye level and pulled the trigger. The bow string snapped forward with a twang and shot the bolt at the dragon. It caught in her ribs.

The dragon dropped her victim and growled in pain as the metal tip embedded itself in her skin. She growled a warning at her attackers.

Vince threw the torch at the dragon. It bounced off her face and she flinched for a second. The torch landed at her feet, the flame still burned brightly. With the dragon dazed, Vince quickly reloaded the crossbow by latching the lever on the bottom back and fired again. This bolt stuck its target in the torso.

A jolt of pain shot though the dragon's body. While they were small, and did not pierce though her tough scales, these weapons were still irritating and painful. A rumbling growl rose up from her throat. Already, she felt the heat rise in her chest as she prepared to use her most deadly weapon. She pulled her head back, inhaled, and unleashed her fire breath.

Orange, yellow, and red flames flew from her mouth in an enormous blaze to engulf her attackers. The fire surrounded them in an intense inferno. The two human wrapped themselves in their cloaks and fell to the ground.

The dragon turned away from the intruders and sprinted towards the light at the mouth of the cave. As she charged out into the open, her wings flared and she thrust herself up into the air. Each down stroke took her higher and further away from the mountain. This place was no longer suited for her to live, the time had come to find a new home.

Chapter 1

Wing beats filled the air as the dragon soared through the cold, cloud filled skies of eastern Romania. Her powerful chest muscles pulsated with each down stroke as they forced her large, leathery wings up and down to stay aloft. With a small shift of her tail, she kept herself on course.

What ever that course was, however, was still a mystery to her. She had come down from her last home in the French Alps to this one in the Carpathian Mountains to escape a trio of dragon slayers that made an attempt on her life. She managed to kill one before retreating, but the other two she was uncertain about. They may have lived, or they may have died. It mattered little to her now, just so long as she was alive herself.

The fierce winds kicked up and she staggered in the air. The dragon flapped her wings hard to steady herself. She managed to regain control of her flight path, but she moved slower now. The wind fought her for every inch she gained.

All the while, even in this storm, she listened. She sought to hear the call of another of her species, another dragon. There were none. The silence deafened her ears, as well as her heart.

In all her life she had only every seen two other dragons; her mother and nest mate, and the last time they were together was almost thirty years ago. She was a thirty-five year old dragon and could easily live for another thirty-five, or even longer. The oldest of her species lived to be well over a century, but those days were long past. The race of dragons had been hunted to the point of near extinction by the only species more cunning and dangerous than herself; humans.

She feared and despised the humans. It was an instinctual fear which had developed deep in the subconscious of every dragon still living on earth, a fear of the two-legged creature.

When man first appeared they were of little interest to the dragons, who had long held dominion over the world. But with the discovery of fire, and later metallurgy, man rose to challenge the once mighty dragon and hunt them for sport.

She knew she could never truly be free of them, her latest encounter was proof enough of that. She still bore the scars from that dragon slayer's weapon on her ribs.

The dragon descended over a crag which jutted out from the mountain side. Her talons latched to the rock and grounded her, pulled her to the earth. The gale force winds bombarded her with snow, which collected in packs on her wings. Snowflakes stung her eyes and clouded her vision. With a growl, she turned into the wind and unleashed a surge of flames in a vain attempt to stop the storm. Fire scorched the air. The snow flakes around her melted and splashed against her scales. But once she stopped, the snow continued to fall and the wind still blew.

As much as she wished to, she could not continue with such a splurging of her fire breath, as the same mechanism that allowed her to breathe fire also let her fly.

The dragon rubbed her body against the rock face to leave her scent. The reason for this was two fold; firstly it was to declare this as her new territory, and secondly it was to attract a mate. Instinct drove her to this, a deep compulsion she did not understand to propagate her race. It was entirely subconscious, as she had never seen a male dragon in her life. Even so, with the odds stacked firmly against her, she was determined.

With her scent markers left, she leapt off the rock and caught the wind. Dipping below the clouds, her wings flared and tail adjusting once again, she headed for her new home.

At the base if the mountain rested a small village. The dragon noticed it when she first came here, but had stayed away as much as she could. She did not want another encounter with the humans, after all. The fact that they lived here was almost a foregone conclusion to her now, they seemed to live everywhere these days. For their part, the humans had not noticed her yet, and she preferred to keep it that way.

***

In the village, a young man stepped out from the local butcher shop with a parcel full of meat slung over his shoulder. He was Richard, the squire and apprentice of the local feudal lord, Sir Ardose.

Once outside, his blonde hair whipped about and his wolf-skin coat fluttered in the wind. With a tug, he readjusted the package of meat and set off for home. The storm was picking up now, most everyone else had retreated inside and were probably sitting comfortably next to their fires.

They were likely all gathered around their hearths, hands reached out towards the flames and fingers tingling in the heat. Their faces aglow in the red warmth. Richard pulled his cloak tighter against this body. The thought of a warm fire just made him feel the cold more fiercely.

His gaze shifted up to the mountain. Even though he had lived his whole life in this village and seen this mountain everyday, the sheer size and majesty of never failed to inspire him. The jagged peaks blanketed white with snow which reached out of the earth.

A flash of orange erupted from the clouds. Richard stopped in his tracks, his feet sank in the snow and quickly started to freeze, but he hardly noticed. What had be just seen? Was that fire? Where did it come from? He squinted his eyes and starred more intently at the mountain top obscured by clouds.

Something burst through from the bottom of the cloud bank. What appeared to be a set of wings flapped as it turned away and flew off towards the mountain. It was faint, little more than a dark shape against the white expanse, but Richard recognized it for what it was. That was a dragon.

Sweat ran down his face and quickly froze in the cold. His fingers were numb, his neck ached from craning his head back, his legs felt weak and watery. Ever since he was a child, Richard had grown up hearing tales of dragons; viscous monsters that burned entire kingdoms to ash and feasted on the flesh of young maidens, and were eventually slain by brave and valiant knights. But he never thought he would see one, even if it was from a great distance.

He wanted to run, needed to run. He needed to warn someone. Anyone. But his legs felt frozen in place. In an act of desperation, he bit down on his lower lip hard enough to draw blood. He broke the fear with pain.

Richard charged off through the village. A spray of snow kicked up behind him as he sprinted. There was only one place he could go, and one man he must tell, Sir Ardose.

The knight lived on the far end of the village in a manor with a nearby barn and a fenced in field for livestock. It was not usually Ardose himself that tended to the animals, but one of the servants.

When Richard reached the house he ran straight to the front door. Wisps of white steam puffed around his face with each breath. His heart pounded and the cold air stung his lungs, he did not care. He pounded his fist against the door repeatedly, and when nothing happened he hit it again.

Richard waited in the cold snow for his lord to appear. Finally, after several anxious moments, a latch shuddered inside and the door pulled inward. Sir Ardose stood in the doorway, dressed in a warm robe with a leather bound book in his hand. Light stubble grew on his cheeks and chin. He pulled a strand of his auburn brown hair away from his eyes. “Richard,” he said, “what is all this ruckus? Did you retrieve the meat like I asked?”

Richard glanced down at the parcel he still clutched tightly. He’d almost completely forgotten about it. "Yes, my lord, I did." He gave a small, customary bow. "But there is something of much greater importance I must tell you." He panted, still working to catch his breath from the sprint over here.

"Well, come inside, then." Ardose shifted to the left. "I'll catch my death in this cold if I stand here much longer."

Richard accepted his lord's invitation, it would have been unwise not to. Inside, he handed the packaged meat off to one of Sir Ardose's servants and hung his cloak on the rack by the door. A fire burned in the stone hearth, the room filled with its heat and dancing light.

Sir Ardose seated himself in a chair by the flames and rested the book over his lap. "Now, my boy, tell me, what was all the commotion about?"

"Sir," Richard spoke, "just now, I believe I saw a dragon."

Ardose's eyes widened. His breathing caught short. Slowly, deliberately, he set the leather bound book on a side table and stood up. "A dragon, you say?"

"Yes, my lord." Richard's arms held tight against his body, his eyes fixed on the floor.

The knight stepped over to the fireplace. He grabbed a poker and nudged the burning coals. Sparks flew up with the smoke. "and when, pray tell, did you see this creature, squire?"

Although his lord's tone was calm and his pose refined, Richard knew of the turmoil which must be boiling underneath. Sir Ardose never refereed to him as ‘squire’ unless something troubled him. “Just now, sir.” He said. “As I was on my way here. I looked up at the sky and saw the creature as it flew down from the mountain. It then disappeared into the clouds.”

“Hm.” Ardose placed the poker back against the rock face of the fireplace. “So, it was flying away when you saw it, is that true?”

“Yes, sir.” Richard nodded.

Ardose starred into the fire. His hands were clasped together behind him and his back was to Richard. “Squire, tell me. What exactly did you see?”

“A dragon, sir.”

“Did you? Is that, in fact, what you saw? Or did you see just some dark shape?” Ardose turned back to face his apprentice. “For all you know, it my not have been anything.”

“But I saw it with my own eyes.” Richard pleaded.

“I do not doubt your conviction.” Ardose said. “But the point I am trying to make is simply that what you thing you saw and what was actually there may not be the same thing.”

Richard kept his arms stiff by his sides. His neck felt hot and his eyes shifted around the room. He was unwilling to meet his master’s gaze. “My lord,” he finally said, “what should we to do?”

“Nothing.” Ardose said in a flat tone.

"Nothing? Sir, with all due respect, there is a fire-breathing dragon now living right on our doorstep, we need to take action to destroy it."

"I admire your bravery, my boy," Sir Ardose spoke, "but I'd like you to think logically for a moment. At this time of year, trying to scout out the mountain would be a dangerous endeavor and only lead to death. And what if we did successfully climb that mountain and found nothing?" Ardose paced in front of the fireplace.

"Is it not better to search in case of a dragon and not find one, than to have a dragon and do nothing?" Richard regretted those words almost as soon as he said them. He'd spoken out of turn and not addressed his master properly. A pit grew in his stomach as he awaited Sir Ardose's response.

"You have made a point." The knight said. "and it is a good point, but think of the villagers. From what you've said, no one else has seen this thing. Rumors of a dragon in these mountains would cause panic and strife among the common people. It is better than we keep this quiet so that the people do not fear. And if there is a dragon, then it will most likely leave soon enough." He stepped over to Richard and looked him straight in the face. "Do you understand?"

Richard gave a quick nod. "Yes, sir."

"Good. Then you are dismissed." Ardose moved back to his chair by the fire.

Richard gabbed the door handle and was about to step out when

Ardose called him back.

"Squire," the knight said, "in the next few weeks I will be going to visit my family and will be away for up to a month. You'll be in charge while I'm gone, and I don't want to hear anymore about this dragon business. Do I make myself clear?"

"Yes, sir." Richard grabbed his cloak off of the rack, slung it over his shoulders, and stepped back into the cold. The wind chilled him down to the bone. He pulled the wolf-skin cloak tighter around him. On impulse, he looked back up at the mountain. He watched and waited. Maybe there would be something else; another flash of fire, another flying dark mass, or even a dragon's roar. But there was nothing.

Perhaps Sir Ardose was right. After all, it was far away and blurry, maybe there wasn't anything after all. Maybe he'd just imagined it.

But still, he was conflicted. With a sigh, he tugged his cloak tightly around him and headed for home, his feet sank into the snow with each step.

But Richard did not think about the snow, he still thought about that thing he saw. What was it? and why did Sir Ardose dismiss him so quickly? Richard frowned. Ardose was the lord and he was his squire, which meant he would follow whatever commands his master told him. Plus, Ardose might be right after all. He would have to wait and see how things turned out.

Chapter 2

The dragon flew down over the tops of the trees, the freshly fallen powder swept into the air as she soared past. She scanned the forest below, her eyes moved back and forth in their sockets. With her wings held out straight to conserve energy, she glided over the forest in search of prey.

A flash of movement caught her attention. An animal took off running below the tree line, its long springy legs propelled it forward in great leaps. The dragon tilted her wings and took off in pursuit. With each down stroke he picked up speed and closed in on her target.

The Last Stand of the Dragon

It was a young doe, not yet old enough to bear fawns. It ran, pushed ahead by its long legs. A fallen tree lay in the deer's path, but it gave an extra push with its hind legs and leapt over it. The doe was fast, but no match for the speed of a dragon's wings.

Each downward thrust of her wings pushed her forward. Faster and faster she flew, the gap between her and her target grew smaller. The branches beneath her blurred together in a mass of green, brown and white as she closed in. A growl formed in her throat. She could almost taste it now.

The trees pulled back as the deer ran into a small clearing. The dragon folded her wings back and fell into a dive. Her front claws reached out, talons like steel hooks prepared to tear flesh. She was eager to catch it, to feel its warm flesh around her claws and blood on her tongue.

As she closed in, her eyesight started to waver. Everything blurred, images turned fuzzy around the edges, an effect of her hunger.

At the last possible second, the deer sprung to the left. It veered off into the trees and left only tiny hoof prints in the snow. Unable to stop her descent, the dragon plowed face first into the snow with an explosion of white powder.

As the snow resettled, the dragon yanked her head back out and shook the remaining snow away. Slightly dazed, and immensely frustrated, she let a vicious growl escape her throat. That growl soon turned into a roar. Even as she roared, her stomach roared just as loud.

This was the third deer to escape her today, and the fourth day since she'd had a successful hunt. Her ribs were noticeably visible on her chest now, and her senses had started to waver. A dragon's eyes were normally sharp enough to spot a deer from more than a mile away at a thousand feet in the air. But it was her vision that had failed her now and let her prey escape.

The animals in this forest were more scarce than they should be, but she did not smell the markings of any other dragons in her territory, or of other large predators like wolves or bears. Never-the-less, something had been hunting in these woods.

The dragon flared her wings and flexed her chest muscles to work out the aches and pains from the crash. She pushed off from the ground, and with a mighty down stroke, was airborne again to begin the hunt anew.

A white haired rabbit jumped through the forest. It raced as fast as its legs could go. The dragon dipped below the tree line and took chase. The small furry animal bounded across the forest floor, its fur blended in perfectly with the snow.

The dragon's eyes began to fade again. The snow, the rabbit, the tree, all of it blurred together. She blinked and shook her head, but when she opened her eyes again, the rabbit was gone.

She banked, the draft of wind caused by her wings kicked up a small burst of snow as she landed. Her eyes shifted from one direction to the other, but there was nothing. Only the standing pines, the blankets of snow all around, and a single fallen log.

Her eyes fixed on the log, a thick black chunk of dead wood against the white of the forest floor. The dragon growled. She charged the tree trunk and slashed it with her claws, the rotten bark splintered and cracked. The startled rabbit raced away from the rotten log towards an open burrow. She took off after it, desperate for food.

This time she would make no mistake. She was too large to fly under the trees, and if the rabbit made another sharp turn it would be impossible for her to keep up, especially in her condition. She had to use her ultimate weapon.

The dragon pushed a gas bubble up from her stomach. Just as it reached the back of her throat, she flexed the pair of venom sacks in the roof of her mouth. Her mouth snapped open, the venom sprayed from her teeth and mixed in the air, it combined with the gas from her stomach and ignited in a stream of fire.

The rabbit's fur instantly set ablaze. It flailed, flopped, and screamed in terrible pain. The dragon closed in and snapped its jaws around the small animal. Bones snapped under the pressure, the rabbit was dead in seconds.

She dropped the flaming carcass back to the snow. The flames extinguished with a hiss of steam. The dragon pawed at her prey. The use of fire on a rabbit was almost a waste of resources, as it was little more than a mouthful to her, and the chemicals needed to produce fire were biologically expensive. What she needed was food, more than just a rodent. She could swallow this whole.

Which is exactly what she did. The dragon took the rabbit in her jaws, tilted her head back, and swallowed it. It may not be much, but she would take anything to quell her hunger.

Chapter 3

"Come along, Rennec." Vince kicked his heels into his horse and the animal trotted forward. His apprentice, Rennec, rode along side on a young gelding. They rode south together to a small township in Northern Italy. A cart was hitched to Rennec's gelding which carried their supplies and weapons. "We are almost there."

"Yes, sir." Rennec whipped the reins.

They came to a small inn on the outskirts of town. After dismounting, Vince handed the reins of his horse to Rennec. "Stay here, I'll secure us a room."

"Yes, sir." Rennec said.

Vince stepped inside the tavern. He found it dimly lit with the innkeeper busy behind the counter and only a few of the tables occupied. "Hmm." He scratched at his beard with a gloved hand. He walked up to the counter and placed his hands firmly on the tabletop. "Excuse me," he said.

The bartender jerked up. He spun around to face Vince and was startled by his appearance; this man dressed like a soldier.

Vince wore his navy blue cape across his shoulders which hung down to his ankles, an armor breastplate over his torso, a pair of thick gloves, and a sword at his hip. His crossbow was slung over his back. "Hello." He spoke with his limited knowledge of Italian. "Need a room. Two people. Stable needed for horses. How much?"

"Ah. A room for two. How long are you expecting to stay?" The inn keeper asked.

"Few days. That is all." Vince said. He pulled open the leather purse on his waist and placed a few gold coins on the counter top. "Is enough?"

The eyes of the inn keeper lit up. He stared at the coins, his face almost illuminated by the reflected light from them. "Yes, yes. Is enough."

"Good." Vince tightened the lacing on his purse and tugged at the strap holding his crossbow in place. "Show me."

Just as the inn keeper was about to direct Vince to the rooms, a loud scream erupted from outside. It was soon joined by other shrieks and shrills as people panicked and started to run. The tavern door flew open and Rennec raced inside. “Sir! It’s a pair of dragons! They’re attacking the village!”

“Oh, no! This can’t be happening, not again!” The inn keeper clasped his hands over his head. He ducked down and crawled under the staircase, curled up in the fetal position.

Vince slid the crossbow off his back and gripped it tightly in his hands. “Rennec, ammunition.”

“Yes, sir.” Rennec ran back outside to the cart and steadied the horses. He climbed inside the cart, quickly found a loading box of quills, and tossed it over to Vince just as the elder man exited the inn.

Vince caught the quills with one hand just before loading them in his crossbow. Overhead, he saw the dragons. It was a pair, one male and one female.

The dragon slayer recognized the differences at a glance. The female was larger, her scales were more dull and pale green, and the horns which grew from the back of her head were shorter and less pronounced. The male was slimmer than his mate, his wings had more reds and yellow in the scales and membranes than the females, his scales were a brighter orange, and his horns were longer and more pronounced.

The male flew over the village. It swooped in low and roared, the villagers ran in terror below. As the dragon neared one building, it unleashed a burst of flames and caught the straw roofing on fire. It then quickly turned away.

Vince recognized exactly what this dragon was doing. This was not hunting behavior, the male was just the distraction. The real threat here was the female. “Rennec, bring my horse.”

Rennec led Vince's horse to him by the reins. Vince quickly hopped on the animals back and kicked it in the sides. “Scout ahead, boy. Find the female, look for the signs like I taught you.” He galloped away before he had a chance to hear the boy’s response. He didn’t need to, he trusted his apprentice.

On horseback, Vince raced through the village, his crossbow at the ready. It didn’t take him long before he spotted the female at a farm, it had just smashed its way into a closed barn and he could hear the animals inside bleating in terror. There was a roar of flames and a snapping of bones. The dragon emerged from the barn with the body of a fully grown ram clamped in her jaws.

Vince tugged on the reins and turned his horse towards the dragon. He latched the lever back on the crossbow, the bowstring pulled back taunt, and a bolt slipped into place. Then, taking his hands off the reins and directing the horse with just his legs, he held the crossbow up at eye level and aimed.

The Last Stand of the Dragon

The female dragon flared its wings, the span of which was nearly twice as wide as its body was long, and took off into the air with a powerful down stroke. The wind kicked up a cloud of dirt around her. Still, Vince's aim was true. He pulled the trigger and the bowstring snapped forward.

The quill flew from the crossbow and struck the beast in the chest. The dragon winced and staggered in the air, but it remained airborne. Vince latched the lever and fired again. This time the bolt struck in the wing joint at the base of the shoulder.

The dragon roared in pain, its prey slipped from its mouth. Unable to flap its wing, the dragon fell back to earth. It crashed with a loud thud to the ground, kicking up a cloud of dust and dirt.

Vince dismounted his horse, he gave it a slap on the flank and it galloped away back to Rennec as it had been trained to. The dust began to settle as Vince approached the fallen creature, his crossbow still gripped firmly in his hands.

The dragon burst from the dust cloud. It charged him with its teeth bared and claws outstretched. A ball of fire escaped from the dragon's open mouth.

Vince ducked to the ground, he pulled his cloak around his body just as the flames engulfed him. He felt the heat, but the fire did not reach him. Once the heat dissipated, he jumped back up and fired the crossbow.

The sharp metal tip of the bolt flew into the dragon's open mouth. It embedded deep in the flesh of its neck and throat. The dragon gagged and coughed, blood gushed from the wound and poured over its tongue to splash on the ground. It snapped its jaws open and shut but couldn't dislodge the intrusion, in fact it only drove the bolt deeper.

As Vince readied another shot, he heard the loud angry roar of the male dragon. It swooped in low over him, a stream of flames erupted from its mouth. Vince covered himself with his cloak as it flew overhead and the fire surrounded him. Sweat poured down his face, he kept his breathing quick and shallow to avoid the smoke.

The female dragon staggered. It gagged on the arrow lodged in its throat, choking on its own blood. The dragon collapsed to the ground, it convulsed and twitched. Its eyes rolled over white as its last breath escaped.

The male landed next to its mate. It nudged the dead female gently with its muzzle, and when that failed it grasped its teeth around the other's neck and tried to lift it up. Try as it might, the male could not revive the dead female.

The dragon slayer threw back his cloak and fired another bolt. This one was a blind shot, and the bolt missed its target completely. The male dragon flinched when the arrow flew past its head. It quickly grabbed the dead goat and took off into the air, leaving its mate and the dragon slayer behind.

Vince watched as the male dragon flew back towards the mountains, chest heaving with excitement and exhaustion. He had not expected to get involved in a dragon hunt today, not that he was complaining. He set the crossbow over his right shoulder and wiped the sweat from his forehead with his left hand.

Vince walked over to the fallen female. It was most likely dead, but he always liked to be sure. Setting the crossbow down gently, he pulled his sword from the sheath, and with a single stroke he beheaded the dragon.

Rennec came riding up on his gelding, the boy held the reins of Vince's horse with his free hand. Vince strode over, he carried the dragon's severed head by one of its horns, and took the reins from his apprentice. "Take this," he said, tossing the head to Rennec.

"Was it the same one?" Rennec asked, now holding the dragon's severed head awkwardly in his lap. "The same female from France?"

"No." Vince mounted his horse. "It had none of the same scars or markings. This was an entirely different female. But this one had a mate, and that means there's likely a nest nearby."

"Chances are good the male is heading that way." Rennec observed.

"Yes. That's true." He snapped the reins and pulled the horse around back to the village. "Come. We should prepare."

No sooner had he turned around then he saw the entire gathering of villagers together in a crowd behind him. They stared at him, awestruck and amazed. A few whispered amongst themselves, and then a person shouted, “He killed the beast!”

“He slayed the dragon!”

The shouts soon erupted into cheers of joy and excitement. The villagers jumped for joy, many hugged one another with delight. A figure emerged from the crowd, a priest dressed in long black robes with a wooden cross hanging around his neck. He bowed deeply to Vince. “You have saved us, Sir knight.” The priest spoke. “Long have we prayed to the Almighty to send us a hero, someone who could save us from these fell beasts, and it is clear that He has sent you to aide us.”

“Trust me,” Vince said in a gravely voice, “God had nothing to do with it. I was just passing through. Where ever dragons are, I go. That’s all.”

“You may think so, but we know in our hearts that it was our Father in Heaven that sent you here. We are in your debt, good Sir knight.”

“If we’re talking debts, then gold will suffice. I usually charge for my services, but if I can get a free room at the inn, I’ll be willing to lower my price.” Vince said.

“Yes, yes, of course. Anything you wish.” The priest replied.

Vince and Rennec rode past the priest and back towards the inn, the crowd parted around them. “and also,” Vince glanced over his shoulder, “I’m no knight.”

Chapter 4

A pale, cone-shaped tooth rested between Vince's thumb and forefinger. He rolled it around in his hand, examining it. Taking a small metal tool, he drilled a hole through the base of the tooth, then pulled the leather string of his necklace through it to add to his collection. "Rennec."

"Yes, sir?" The boy finished tying off the bag which held the dragon's head and placed it in the back of the cart.

"Did you get a baring on where the male dragon flew?" Vince slipped the necklace back over his head, the dragon's teeth rested against his armor breastplate.

"Yes, sir."

"Good." Vince took a rag and wiped down his sword. It was still covered with dragon blood and he needed to get it cleaned off as soon as possible before the blade rusted. Once the sword was clean, he sheathed it. "Then we should be on the move again, before that dragon has a chance to escape."

"So soon, sir?" Rennec asked as he stepped down from the cart. "Shouldn't we rest? We just got here and haven't even unpacked for the night."

"They were a breeding pair, which means there's a nest." Vince explained. "And since they were gathering food together, it's likely those eggs are going to hatch soon. The longer we wait, the less time we have before they do." He remounted his horse, his feet slipped through he stirrups. "We move immediately."

"Yes, sir." Rennec loaded up his gelding with the supplies they'd need. An unlit torch, two pieces of flint, a box of ammunition for the crossbow, and a pair of small axes.

As they were about to leave the village, the town priest and a small number of villagers approached them. The priest waved them down. "Sir knight, wait a moment, please."

"I told you, I am not a knight." Vince said.

"Some of the men wish to join you on the hunt." The priest motioned to the men behind him. All peasant farmers, most holding pitchforks or axes. “Their homes and families have been destroyed by the dragons, will you allow them to go with?”

“Please, mister dragon slayer. We want that monster dead more than anything. Please, let us go with you.” One of the farmer’s, a peasant boy no older than Rennec, begged.

Vince closed his eyes. He recognized the desperation on their faces, as he had seen it many times before. It was the same look Rennec gave him after a dragon burned down his home and made him an orphan, and the same look Vince once had himself.

“I know the grief that you feel,” he said, “but I can’t let you follow me. This is not a simple hunt for deer or boar, or even bear. This is a dragon, and when hunting dragons even the most experienced don’t always escape unscathed.” He traced a finger down a scar on his face. The scar began above his right eyebrow, curved around his eye, cut through his cheek, followed the jaw line, and finally came to an end all the way at the cleft of his chin.

“Then,” the priest clasped his hands together. “At least allow us to pray for your safety.”

“I’m sure God has His uses.” Vince said. “But killing dragons is one of mine. Let’s go, Rennec.” He snapped the reins and gave a kick. His horse trotted forward.

Vince and Rennec rode side by side in silence up the rocky mountain trail. After a while, the trail ended and they took the horses onto more uneven terrain. Eventually, even that was too much for them and they had to dismount and continue on foot.

As they rode, and later hiked, up the gravely slopes, the faces of the villagers continued to linger in Vince's mind. The deep set eyes, scraggly faces, unkempt beards. The sorrow that flowed out from those eyes, and deeper than that was rage. Rage at the dragons, or rage at the Creator for sending the dragon.

Vince didn't believe that any Creator sent these beasts. To him, it was just a monster that needed to be exterminated. He traced his finger along the scar over his face again, a permanent reminder of his first encounter with a dragon.

"I can see a cave, sir." Rennec's voice alerted him.

They crawled up behind a pair of large rocks, Vince pressed his back against one and reloaded the crossbow. He peeked around the edge of the jagged rock to see the dark cavern stretching back into the mountain. "Rennec," Vince said, his voice barely over a hushed whisper, "stay low and wait out here for me."

"Yes, sir."

Just as Vince stood and began his advance towards the cave, the male dragon appeared. It came charging out, wings fully stretched. Vince barely had time to duck as the dragon took off. It leapt into the air, causing a gust of wind from its wings. Vince spun around and came to a crouched stance, one knee planted in the earth, and he fired a bolt at the fleeing dragon.

He missed. The dragon did not turn back to fight, nor did it head towards the village. Instead, it veered off to the east. By the time Vince had the crossbow notched back into place, the dragon was out of range.

Vince dusted himself off as he stood. He unlatched the bowstring, swung the crossbow over his shoulder, and signaled for Rennec to emerge.

"What happened, sir?" Rennec asked.

"I cannot say. I guess it knew we were coming and chose to abandon its home rather than face us." Vince placed his hand on Rennec's shoulder. "You did well, today. You followed his trail and lead me to him excellently. Your tracking skills have improved." He gave a smile, one Rennec gladly returned. Vince then motioned to the cave. "Come along, we still have a job to do."

Rennec took the torch and lit it with the flint. He handed it to Vince, who then proceeded into the cavern. With the flaming branch held out before him, the dragon slayer drew his sword .

Together, they walked down the dark passage of the cave until they came to the end chamber. Inside, they found a cone-shaped pile of stones with sticks and leaves burning around it. Inside the pile of rocks there sat two eggs, each as large as a horse's head. A dragon's nest.

Rennec starred awestruck at the glowing rock pile. This was the first time he had ever seen a dragon nest. “Why do they burn their eggs?”

“Dragons can’t sit on eggs like birds. They pile up the rock and breath fire on them to keep them warm.” Vince explained. “Temperature determines whether a dragon hatchling is male or female. Hotter for males, colder for females.”

“What are we going to do with them?” Rennec asked.

Vince handed the torch over to his apprentice. Then, with grim determination, he kicked the nest. Rocks tumbled to the side and the eggs rolled out onto the cold cave floor. The dragon slayer sheathed his sword, knelt down beside the first egg, then grabbed one of the larger base rocks with his gloved hands and lifted it over his head. “We smash them.” He brought the rock down hard on the egg. The shell shattered.

Chapter 5

Dennis was a young lad, only thirteen years old, but stronger than other boys as old as sixteen. His father died when he was only nine and left him as the man in his family's house. The boy was no farmer, and had no skills as a masonry worker or craftsman.

What he was good at was hunting. Before his father died, the two of them went on hunting trips together and Dennis was taught how to kill a deer with a bow, and also how to skin it, tan the hide, and prepare the meat. Through this skill as a hunter and fur trader, he was able to feed his mother and sister.

It was here that he found himself trudging through the woods in ankle deep snow. Each time he took a step he had to yank his foot from the snow only to have it sink back down in front of him. He was layered in animal furs to keep warm and had a quiver of arrows slung across his back.

He held his father's bow out before him, just in case he found something. For a while now he'd been following the trail of a deer. It was a young deer by the shapes of the hooves, maybe a buck just after shedding its first set of antlers.

Dennis soon came upon the deer. He watched it from a little less than a hundred yards away as the buck nibbled at the beech nuts of low branches.

Hiding behind a tree, Dennis drew an arrow from the quiver and latched the end into the bowstring. This wasn't the largest deer he'd killed out here, but it would bring food for a while and he could sell the skin. He peeked around the tree trunk and lined up his shot.

He released his grip on the taunt string. The arrow launched forward, struck the deer through the ribs, and pierced the heart.

The buck jumped in the air, its legs flailed sporadically before they caught under its body and it took off running. Dennis watched as it sprang through the trees. There was no need to chase it, that was a kill shot. All he needed to do was follow the trail of blood left in the snow.

Less than twenty-five yards from where he shot it, Dennis found the deer's body. It lay motionless in the snow which had turned red from its blood. Dennis felt an immense sense of pride within himself. There was always a level of joy after a successful hunt, an accomplishment and satisfaction that he was a man, even if he was much younger than his fellows.

He unstrung his bow, slipped it into the quiver along with the used arrow, then, with his greater than average for his age strength, lifted the deer's body across his shoulders. The going was slower than before, but he was headed for home with his prize.

A shadow passed over him. He stopped dead in his tracks, the deer weighed heavily on his back. There was a whoosh as the shadow flew over again. He watched as the dark shape circled around him, growing larger.

Dennis' fear grew as did the shadow. He slowly tilted his head back as far it he could and shifted his eyes for the sky. That's when he saw it. The dragon.

***

The female dragon had been surveying her territory for prey, as she did most everyday. She'd spotted the young buck and was preparing to attack it when the animal was instead struck down by the human hunter. At least now she knew why food was harder to find out here.

The Last Stand of the Dragon

Scavenging was not unusual for a dragon. If need be, she would scare off a bear or a pack of wolves from a kill. This would be no different than that.

She swooped down upon the human, her claws were outstretched and teeth bared. Her roar was ear splitting. The human boy screamed, although neither he nor the dragon could hear his voice over the roar. He threw himself to the ground and covered his head with both hands, shivering in terror.

The dragon banked with her powerful wings, the wake kicked up a cloud of snow around her. She landed over the human boy cowering below her, her feet planted in the snow on both sides of his body. She had no real interest in him, she merely wanted the animal draped over his back.

Her jaws latched tightly around the deer carcass, bones snapped under the pressure. She lifted it with ease off the boy. Then flared her wings and took off again, heading back to her cave.

***

Dennis lay face down in the snow, his fingers laced together behind his head, as he waited for the dragon to attack. His heart raced, and although he wasn't trying to, he wept like a child. He'd heard the stories after all; a monstrous dragon would fly down and kill a man in a heartbeat, strike him down with one swing of its claws, or maybe burn him alive in fire.

But nothing happened. Instead, all he felt was the weight of the deer lift off his back, followed by the beating of the dragon's wings as it flew away with his family's food.

As the wing beats grew fainter, Dennis slowly unlaced his fingers and looked up. He saw the footprints deep in the snow from were the dragon had stood, and looking over his shoulder he saw the creature itself as it flew away, but he was unharmed.

It must have been a sign. God had been watching him and made the beast leave, that was the only explanation. God wanted him to live, to warn the rest of his village about this monster on their doorstep.

With a new sense of urgency, Dennis pushed himself up and started to run as fast as he could. His legs burned and lungs aches as he plowed through the snow, but he trudged on. He had to reach his village, he had to warn Sir Ardose.

He soon spotted the village. As he approached, he saw a lone man on a horse. He soon saw it was Sir Ardose himself. He came running up, waving his arms over his head and shouting. "Sir! Sir! My lord!"

Ardose saw the young man coming towards him and halted his horse. The boy's run slowed to a slow jog and finally stopped completely as he came up next to the knight. Dennis, exhausted from his run, doubled over with his hands placed on his knees, and breath forming clouds around his face.

"You have something important, child?" Ardose said. "I have an appointment to keep and only a day to travel, I don't have long to talk."

"My lord," Dennis sputtered between gasps, "I've . . . just been . . . attacked . . . by a dragon."

Sir Ardose's eyebrow perked up. His interest and concerns were piqued. "A dragon, you say?" He said, his hands rung the reins of his horse. "Where did this happen?"

"In the woods. Just off to the north that way." Dennis pointed back at the trench through the snow he'd just made. "I was hunting when it came down out of the sky and attacked me."

"Show me where." Sir Ardose demanded.

"Yes, my lord." Dennis said. "Do you mean right now?"

"Of course I do." Ardose snapped the reins and turned the horse towards the forest. "Lead on, boy."

Dennis' heart began to swell. Not only had he escaped the wrath of a fire-breathing dragon, but now he had been ordered by the lord of his village to lead a quest against this monster.

Maybe, he though, Ardose might make him a page for his services, and maybe even eventually a new squire. Sir Ardose's current squire, Richard, was most certainly old enough and skilled enough to be knighted himself, and if Dennis was made an apprentice to the local lord, then all the problems his family faced would be gone. His mother and sister would always have warm clothes and plenty of food on the table during the cold winters.

He was so lost in his thoughts that he found himself upon the site of his encounter before he realized it. Dennis looked down on the depression in the snow where he had once lain, and the deep footprints left by the dragon. "Here it happened, sir." Dennis said. "I was laying right here and the beast stood over me."

"Yes, I see." Ardose dismounted his horse. He knelt by the impressions in the snow, his hand rested on his chin. "And the creature did you no harm?"

"It tried, sir." Dennis said. The embellishment part of his young boy mind was starting to get the better of him. "I had my father's arrows with me and as it tried to attack, I pulled one out and stabbed at its face. The monster never saw it coming."

"No, I suppose it didn't." Ardose said. Dennis never had time to notice the knife in Ardose's hand before it plunged into his back.

Chapter 6

Richard stared up at the steeple of the church. In this small village, the church was the largest single structure, capable of housing potentially everyone in the village. The base was built of stone held together with mortar, while everything above the doors was made of wood. The bell rang out from the tower overhead. Today was not service, but still Richard had a strong conviction to go inside.

With a heavy sigh, he entered. While snow was falling outside, the inside of the church was warm. The pews were lined along the sides to

face the podium at the front. Candles were alight, casting their faint warm glow throughout the chapel.

Stained-glass windows lined the walls, depicting images of the saints and of the virgin Mary. One window that caught Richard's attention immediately was of a knight on horseback, dressed in full armor, stabbing a lance into the heart of a dragon.

To one side of building was the confessional booth. That was Richard's destination. He stepped up to it, rested his knees on the bench, and made the sign of the cross over his chest. "Bless me, Father, for I have sinned."

"The Lord is with thee, child." The voice of the priest came from the other side of the curtain. "Confess your sins and they shall be forgiven."

"I am in doubt, Father. I have been asked to keep a secret, but I do not know that I can."

"What secret, my child?" The priest asked.

Richard explained. "I saw something the other day, and my lord, Sir Ardose, asked that I keep it a secret from the rest of the village. I don't know why he's asked this of me. Father, if someone asked you to keep a deep secret, would you be able to?"

The priest's voice came from behind the curtain again. "My child, you are young. People come to me with their sins, and regardless of what those sins are, once they are confessed with a broken heart and a broken spirit, the Lord forgives them and remembers no more. I am asked to keep secrets all the time."

Richard nodded.

"Sir Ardose has asked you this important thing. Whether you share that with me is not important." The priest continued. "He is your lord, and he has asked this of you. You must have faith in his wisdom. Do you understand?"

He understood, but Richard was not reassured by the priests words. Some part of him wanted to be told otherwise, that he needed to inform the people of the potential danger. He'd hoped the priest would give him instruction to follow his own instincts. "I hear you, Father."

"Your sins are forgiven. Go forth and sin no more."

Richard stood up from the confessional. As he walked back towards the door, he glanced at the windows one more time. His eyes fixed on the one of the knight and dragon. As he stared at the dragon, the lance piercing through its chest and red blood pouring out, Richard could almost hear the whinnying of the horse, the clatter of the knight's armor, and the roars of the dragon.

He shuddered, pulled his coat tighter, and stepped out into the cold. As he walked through the village, small flakes of snow falling from the clouds which blanketed the sky, he looked by up at the mountain. It had been three days since he glimpsed the dragon, and since then nothing has happened. No sightings, no reports, nothing. Perhaps Sir

Ardose was right. The dragon, or whatever it was he saw that day, was likely long gone by now, if it was even there to begin with.

In any case, this was not for him to worry about. He was only a squire, after all, not a lord or knight. Should the day come when Sir Ardose saw fit to knight him, then he could worry about the possible dangers of flying fire-breathers.

Sir Ardose, however, was away visiting with his family in another township many miles away. Richard didn't know how long he would be gone, but the point remained that Ardose has left the village and Richard did not know when he would return.

The more Richard thought, the more anxious be became. What he really needed right now was something to calm his nerves, and he knew the best place to do that.

He came to the local tavern. A sign hung above the door which creaked on its rusted hinges as the wind blew. It read, *The Roaring Lion*. He pushed the door open and a wave of heat flooded out to greet him. A fire burned and roared in the fireplace, it cast its dim, warm light across the room. People sat around the many circular tables talking and laughing. Some folks drank ale, others had beer, a few had wine, whatever their hearts content.

Richard closed the door tightly behind him, listening for it to latched shut. He pulled his wolf-skin coat off and placed it on the rack by the door.

The bartender, Abel, stood behind the counter with a rag in his hand as he wiped down the glasses. He was a short man, balding on top and round in the middle, but with a friendly face. When he was Richard by the door, he set the glass down and waved, a huge smile across his face. "Richard! Come on over."

Richard did as he was beckoned. He set himself down at the counter, his elbows rested on the wood surface. "Hi, Abel."

"Boy, how you doing? I haven't seen you in a while." Abel filled a glass halfway with ale from one of the five wood barrels behind the counter. He set it down at Richard's hands.

"I haven't been feeling so well, actually." Richard pushed the glass back. "If you could, can you fill that up all the way? I have a lot on my mind right now."

"All the way?" Abel took back the glass and filled it to the top. "That's a whole pint, I've never known you to drink more than a half at a time."

"Again, I have a lot to think about." Richard Took the mug of ale and pressed the rim to his lips. He drank half of it at once before setting the glass back down. "I can never figure out how this stuff tastes so bad and yet so good at the same time."

"That would be my little secret." Abel replied.

A loud crash caught Richard's attention. He turned around and saw one of the local farmers, Phillip, laying on his back, drenched from head to toe in beer. He'd just been joking and laughing with another farmer, William, when he'd leaned too far back and fell over.

Everyone in the tavern starred at him in silence just before erupting in a chorus of laughter. Phillip rolled away from his chair and crawled around on his hands and knees. Drunk and blind as a bat, his hand eventually found the now empty mug of beer with draggles of yellowish foam still clinging to it. He held it up over his head. "Hey, barman!" He shouted. "Pour me another!" His words slurred lazily together.

Abel leaned on the counter and shot an annoyed look at the poor fellow on his floor. "I think you've had too much already, Phil."

Phillip did not listen. The sounds of his snoring was too loud. He had fallen into an alcohol induced sleep, drool oozed from his mouth. Richard sighed and shook his head. "Now he's drooling all over the floor."

"I'm just grateful it's only drool this time." Abel said with a smile. "I hope his wife's coming to get him, because I'm not carrying him home again." He grabbed the towel again and began to wipe down the counter. "Hey, Richard, I don't suppose you know how long Sir Ardose will be away."

Richard shook his head. "He didn't tell me exactly. Up to a month. Just visiting the family, I guess."

Abel nodded with agreement. "That's always a nice thing to do."

Chapter 7

Even as Richard and Abel talked about him, Ardose rode his horse through the streets of the nearby township. He had family that did indeed live in this town, but that was not the only reason he was here, not was it the most important one. At least, not anymore.

When he left the village three days ago, his only plan was to visit with his sister and her husband and children, but when that peasant boy (Ardose had to think hard to remember his name was Dennis) approached him on his way out of town, the plans changed.

The Last Stand of the Dragon

Ardose believed Richard's story about the dragon, but also thought it likely had moved on. So when the peasant boy came to him with claims of encountering it up close, Ardose knew that would not be leaving anytime soon. Armed with this knowledge, he began to formulate a plan in his mind.

Sir Nathaniel Ardose was the third born son of a lower noble and had been knighted at the young age of seventeen. He inherited one small portion of his father's lands. As a boy he'd always envied the status and wealth of a knight, and all the power and nobility that came with it, and the adventures that knights got to partake in. He wished to travel and go on quests for treasure or a glorious fight with trolls or ogres, whatever monsters he could imagine. When his father died and he received his knighthood, he envisioned all the glory that would come with it.

What he didn't expect, however, was all the responsibilities that also came with being a knight. All the times he had to answer to other lords of greater status than himself, and every time he needed to sort out a dispute between the peasants that lived on his land. He spent less time jousting or fighting and more time squalling at those lesser than himself. His position had brought him nothing but grief, deeper wrinkles and grayer hair. Long gone were the days when he dreamed of adventure.

But now with the dragon, he saw a chance to escape it all. And that was why he stabbed the peasant boy in the back and left him to die in the snow. His plan required that the dragon remained a secret for as long as possible. So he couldn't have that boy going around town telling everyone what he'd seen.

Ardose dismounted his horse when he arrived at his destination. This was the real reason he came to this township, a figure legendary for his dragon slaying abilities. Cain.

He tied his horse to a post and stepped inside the small hut shaped building. Inside was a large room lit only by the light of a single candle, which itself stood on the corner of a single desk. The flame flickered as the wind rushed in from outside. The desk was covered with piles of paper.

A solitary figure sat behind the desk with a feather quill pen between his long, bony fingers. The quill moved rapidly across the page, a trail of ink left in its wake. Thin, stringy hair lay atop the figure's otherwise bald head. Ardose slammed the door shut behind, and the figure's head jolted up.

For the first time, Ardose saw the man's face. His skin was thin and taunt, like it was pulled tight against his skull. His cheekbones jutted out from under his eyes, and his brows dipped in the center as if he was giving a permanent glare. His icy-blue eyes starred intensely back in the darkness. When Ardose saw those eyes, a shiver ran up his spine. "Are you Cain?"

"What do you want?" The man in the dark growled. His voice as deep and gravely as a bone bed.

Ardose cleared his throat. "Oh, nothing . Probably nothing of much important to a man like yourself."

"Then, if you don't mind, kindly leave me to my peace. I wish to rot in silence." Cain grumbled. His eyes never left Ardose.

Those eyes, something about them just did not sit well with Ardose. Cold and merciless, the only thing he saw in Cain's eyes was evil. Still, he was here for a reason.

"The truth of the matter is I'm looking to hire someone. I have a job needs doing for someone with particular skills. Skills, I am told, you possess." Ardose said. "Perhaps, a dragon that needs slaying?"

Cain placed the feather quill down and laced his long, knobby fingers together. "I'm listening."

"Good." Ardose stepped deeper into the dark room. "But, before I tell you anything else, I want to make a deal with you."

"What kind of deal?" Cain asked, he lifted a single eyebrow in concern. "Do you want a cut of the fee? That won't happen." He looked away from Ardose, grabbed the pen and continued writing. "I'd rather watch your precious village burn then give you any gold."

Ardose let out a small chuckle. "As a matter of fact, that's exactly what I want."

Cain's pen stopped mid-sentence. A black spot of ink formed on the page. His eyes shifted back to the knight. "Excuse me? I'm not sure I heard that right."

Ardose walked up to the desk and placed both his hands down firmly. "It's true, I want that dragon slain, just as any rational man would. But, not before it turns that speck of a village to ash."

Cain pushed himself up from the chair. His face was illuminated from below by the dim light of the candle casting shadows over his eyes. "That's one of the more unusual requests I've heard. May I ask why?"

"Because I want out." Ardose said. "I don't want to be their warden anymore. Those thankless peasants always come to me with all their petty squabbles and disjointed lives. I'm sick of it. I'd much rather be an adventurer, go out on my horse and never look back, maybe be a mercenary. But the image of honor prevents me from just leaving."

"If you want to go on adventures and live a life of freedom, why not just slay the dragon yourself?" Cain snidely replied.

"I need a man with experience." Ardose said. "And besides, if I'm to leave that ash pile once it's all over, I'll need plenty of coin in my purse."

"I see. So you do want a cut." Cain set himself back down and took up the pen. "If you're here trying to worm some money out of me, then who's back with your precious sheep to make sure they don't get eaten before you can sentence them to death?"

"My squire is there. He's rather skilled with a sword, I trained him myself." Ardose said. "Besides, we can fleece that flock of sheep of every coin they have. It's far more than your usual rate, even split in half between us. You have much to gain from this venture."

Cain leaned back in the chair, his pointed fingernail scratched at the wooden surface of his desk.

This knight was a sly little rat he had before him, and not exactly a stupid one. If Cain had a choice, he'd rather make dealings with a clever trickster than an honest fool. "Very well. I can play along with your schemes," he finally spoke, "has anyone other than you or your squire witnessed the beast firsthand?"

"Only a peasant boy, but he won't be telling anyone else." Ardose replied.

"And why is that?"

"It's difficult to talk when you have a knife in your back."

A grin crept across Cain's face as he stared at Ardose. That grin made the hair on the back of Ardose's neck stand on end. In the dimly lit room, that smile combined with his bony face, deep set eyes, jutting cheek bones, and dipping brow gave Cain the appearance of a monster. Like he was the devil himself. It send a shiver running down the length of Ardose's spin and for a moment, he wondered what exactly he was getting into.

"I guess I can consider your plan." Cain finally said. "However, you'll need to wait. The dragon must reveal itself to the people. Once it does, then the people will be willing to pay virtually anything to be rid of it." He placed his hands together in front of his face. "But we must be patient, my devious friend. Patience is a virtue, after all."

Chapter 8

The male dragon flapped his wings. He stained with each down stroke. He must keep flying, has to keep going. They might still be after him. Although time had past since his mate's death and the later attack on his cave, the image of his mate laying on the ground and choking on her own blood still lingered in his mind.

The female should have just left the ram and flown away, then at least she'd have survived. But she wasn't as smart as him, or her maternal instincts were too strong. He knew that she was driven to feed her young when they hatched, but once she was dead he abandoned the nest and saved his own skin. They could have easily lain more eggs, but instead she died trying to feed and protect it. It was her own fault the female died.

But that image still burned fresh in his mind; her body laying cold on the ground with a bolt sticking out of her mouth and blood pooling around her head. He shook his head violently back and forth, as if the memory was a thorn lodged in his mind that he could remove if he tried hard enough. But he could not forget her death rattles.

A fierce wind struck the male dragon from the east. He wobbled in the air as he tried to regain his balance. His tail stiffened and he tilted his wings. He was about to turn away from the wind when he caught an erotic and enticing scent; the scent of a female in heat. The smell was coming from the mountains to the east.

He returned to his previous course and flew towards those mountains. If there was anything that could distract a male dragon from the horrors of his previous affiliation's fate, it would be a female ready and willing to mate.

The female rested at the mouth of her cave. Snow had already fallen in these mountains, there never seemed to be a time without it. She lay on the ground with her wings fully extended to catch the warmth of the sun. The skies were clear aside from a few white, fluffy clouds. The storms that usually blanketed the mountaintops seemed to be resting as well. Her eyelids were heavy and drooped lower as time wore on. In a few minutes she would be asleep.

A loud and tremendous roar broke the silence. She jolted up from her near slumber and looked around in confusion,now at full alert. That roar sounded familiar, and yet alien at the same time. She'd never heard one like it, but instinctively knew the source.

There was another roar as the animal that made it came into vision. She recognized it instantly, even though she'd never seen one. It was a male dragon.

He was slimmer than her, his scales were a bright orange with hints of red and yellow in his wings, and the horns on he head were more pronounced than hers. It was unbelievable. Against all odds, he had heard her mating calls.

The male flew in a circular pattern over her. He unleashed a burst of flames as he did. This was a show of force and of confidence in himself that he would use a resource as precious as fire on mere display.

She was enamored by him. In all her life she had never seen a male dragon until now, and to her he was amazing. The female flapped her wings in preparation, and then with a mighty push of her legs, she became airborne. Her powerful chest muscles pulsated, her heart pounded in her chest to deliver oxygen rich blood. She tilted her wings and moved in closer to the male.

He, too, adjusted his flight pattern. The two dragons began to circle one another, they slowly ascended in a gradual upward spiral. The female's eyes never left him, even while in midair.

Her heart was pounding, harder that it usually did while flying. What that normal? Was there something about this male that was confusing her mind? Why was she so transfixed on him?

They flew around each other until they reached the underside of the clouds. Water droplets splattered against their scales, the two hardly noticed. The mating dance continued, and the circle tightened. Her head swam with thoughts and emotions, so much happening to her at once. Her heart raced so fast she was almost afraid it would burst.

Just then, when they were within wingtip distance of each other, the male reached out with his hind claws. She reciprocated and together they locked talons. Then, they folded their wings and started to fall.

They plummeted head first towards the earth below, spinning as the air rushed past their bodies. They pulled each other closer and latched their front claws together as well. The ground grew closer and closer, but they took no notice. All thoughts had left their minds; they had become one creature, no longer separate entities.

At the last possible second, they released their hold on one another, flared their wings, and flew apart. As the dragons took a sharp turn away from the ground, the female blasted a stream of fire from her mouth. It scorched the rocks and snow beneath her. Trust had been earned between them, the female was now willing to mate. With the union of these dragons came a glimmer of hope for he survival of the species.

***

Richard placed a hand against his forehead and rubbed his temples. His head throbbed, as if a spike was being driven into it. His vision swirled with images and he staggered on his feet.

Chopping logs for firewood was not a great idea when one is suffering the effects of Day-After-Drinking, but it was a job he still had to do. He propped himself up on the blunt end of his axe while trying to regain his composure. A slight groan escaped his lips. He knew he shouldn't have drunk so much yesterday.

Abel was right, he must be the cheapest drunk in the world if little more than a pint did this to him. Of course, Phillip and those guys drank at least three or four a day. Richard would be more surprised if he ever saw them sober.1

The only reason he'd gone to the tavern immediately after his confession was to clear his mind. The priest's words helped, but not as much as he hoped. Ever since he saw it, all Richard could think about was that dragon thing. Sir Ardose's told him not to speak of it, and so far he hasn't, not even to the priest during confession, and amazingly not while drunk yesterday. But even now with e pulsing headache, he mind still went back to flapping wings and blazing flames.

Someone should know. He seriously felt this was so important he would defy the wishes of his lord if it meant possibly saving people, and he would've if not for the priest's reassurance. He wanted to tell the people, wanted to warn them about the fire-breathing monster that now inhabited their mountain, or at least inform them of his suspicions. Besides, if Ardose was right and the dragon was long gone by now, then there was no real harm in telling anyone, right?

He became so wrapped up in his thoughts he didn't see the person approaching him until they were standing literally right beside him. "Richard? Hello? Are you feeling alright?"

"Huh?" He looked up and found himself staring directly into the emerald-green eyes of Rachel. "Oh, Rachel." He said. He hurriedly straightened himself out, pushed his chest out and held his chin up. "I'm sorry, I didn't see you there." His cheeks flushed pink.

"You didn't hear me very well, either." A coy smile peeked up at the corners of Rachel's lips. "I've been calling your name for the past few minutes. Is everything okay?"

Richard cleared his throat. "Oh, yeah. Never better. Why do you ask?"

"You don't seem to be here. I mean, you're standing in front of me, of course, but your mind seems to be far away in a different place." Rachel said. A light breeze picked up and rustled her wavy, fire-red hair.

"Sorry," Richard said, "I'm just recovering from Day-After-Drinking. Thought maybe chopping for firewood for the winter would help settle my mind."

"I'd assume it's dangerous to swing an axe while still re-covering from Day-After-Drinking." Rachel quipped. "Actually, I'm here to talk about my brother."

"Dennis?" Richard asked. "Yes, I've met the boy, a good lad. How is he doing?"

"I don't know, he's been missing for days."

"Days?" Richard asked. "Doesn't he normally go hunting? People can be out for a while on a hunt."

"Not Dennis." Rachel shook her head, a look of concern over her face. "He'd never be gone for this long. I'm worried that something might have happened to him, but with Sir Ardose away I didn't know who else to turn to other than you."

Richard nodded. "I see. I'll do what I can. Tomorrow I'll organize a search to go looking for him. I can't guarantee anything, but I will try."

Rachel gave a sweet smile and bow lightly. "Thank you, Sir."

"You don't need to call me that, my lady. I am not a knight."

"And I am not a true lady, either." She chuckled. "Thank you, once again. It means a lot to me."

"I'm glad I can help." Richard took her hand and kissed it. Her face turned almost as red as her hair. She turned and started walking away. Richard returned to his wood chopping.

Dennis was missing, and now his sister was concerned for his safety. These thoughts weighed heavily on Richard's mind. He's never spent much time with the younger boy, but he knew Dennis could handle a bow and arrow effectively, probably even better than himself.

A terrible idea formed in his head. He stopped his axe mid-swing. Rachel had said her brother went missing while hunting in the woods. What if Dennis was attacked by the dragon while hunting in the mountains?

He set the axe down and was about to call back to Rachel, but stopped himself. Richard felt it better not to disturb her. He grabbed his axe again and brought it down on the chunk of wood.

Chapter 9

A cone shaped pile of rocks, sticks, wood, and leaves smoldered within a cave in the mountain. The female dragon stood over it, she watched with intently undivided attention. Was it the right temperature, or was it too cold? She opened her mouth and a burst of flames scorched the rocks.

Gingerly, the dragon pushed a single rock aside and looked inside. Two large, oval-shaped, off-white objects rested inside the burning mound. They were her eggs.

Only three days had past since she mated with the male, and already she had laid the eggs. This pile of rocks and debris was her nest to keep them warm in these freezing mountains. The rocks protected the eggs from any predators, (although that was very unlikely in the depths of a dragon's lair) and shielded the eggs from a direct blast of fire. They also acted as miniature heaters, absorbing heat from the fire as it burned and then releasing it slowly back onto the eggs. The female knew through instinct that if the nest became too cold her eggs would die, and this she would not allow.

She heard a flutter of leathery wings approach from outside the cave. She turned towards the sound, her lips curled back and teeth bared. A growl rumbled in her throat. She must be cautious. This was her first brood, and she would not allow any harm to come to it. If it was required of her, she would die, or kill, for her eggs. Nothing was allowed near her nest without her approval, and getting that was not easy. She blasted the nest with another burst of fire, and then crept to the entrance of her cave.

The male dragon settled to the ground outside the cave, his wings folded tight against his body. He'd just returned from a hunt, an unsuccessful hunt at that, while the female guarded the nest. She would not be pleased with this, but it was unavoidable. Food was already scarce in these mountains before he arrived, two mature adult dragons was greater than this ecosystem could support.

Had he returned with nothing to show, the least the female would do is banish him from her domain. The worst case scenario would be her tearing his throat out while he was still alive. Fortunately, he had anticipated this and brought something he hoped would appease her.

She emerged from the cave entrance, stepping out of the darkness and into the light. She glared intently at the male expectantly. She was larger than him and heavier by about five hundred pounds, in a fight there would be no contest. The male backed away with his head dipped low in a submissive stance. He dropped a smoldering lump from his mouth. The female inspected it, nudging it with her snout.

Another rock for the nest.

The female looked down at the rock, then back up at the male. After a moments hesitation, she stepped aside and allowed entrance. The male scooped the rock back up with his mouth and cautiously entered the cave, the female's eyes never left him for a second. Only once he disappeared completely in the cave did the female spread her wings and take off. Now it was her turn to hunt, and his turn to guard the nest.

The male walked through the cave until he came to the smoking pile of rocks. He dropped the new stone on top of the others. He sniffed at the nest, inspecting it. Instinct told him it was too warm. Just like the female was driven to keep the nest warmer, he was driven to cool it down. The warmer a nest, the more likely the eggs would produce males, while the cooler it was the better likelihood for female hatchlings. Any other male dragon, even a son, would compete with him for territory, food, and mates.

Slowly, only a few at a time, he started to pull rocks off the nest. The life-giving heat flowed away from the nest as each stone was removed. The temperature steadily dropped. He would make sure to remove any potential rivals before they could even hatch. However, in doing so, the warmth that kept the embryos alive in these freezing mountains diminished.

The female returned the next day from yet another unsuccessful hunt. She flared her wings and banked to land, the wind kicked up a cloud of fresh powdery snow. They male lay at the mouth of the cave, waiting for her.

That was not right. He should be inside with the nest, what was he doing out here? Immediately, she could tell something was wrong. Terribly wrong. As the male woke and stood to greet her, she snarled, her teeth bared. The male backed away with his head held low.

The female charged past him into her cave. She ran until she came to the nest. Her fears were confirmed. Rocks were scattered all around, the fire inside had burned down to only a few small embers. And one of the eggs had been smashed open, the broken pieces of shell lay scattered across the floor. The baby dragon embryo, mostly formed, lay cold and motionless in a pool of the egg yoke.

No! She would not let her first clutch die! The female let out a screaming roar, a blast of fire erupted from her maw and engulfed the remains of the nest, reigniting the embers. The second egg was still intact, and might survive. This, however, was a moot point for her. The male had not only neglected the nest, he had deliberately killed one of her babies, and this she would not tolerate.

She charged back out of the cave in full rage attack mode. The male was caught by surprise when she pounced on him, her claws and teeth tore into his skin. He roared in pain as her fangs sank into the soft flesh around his throat.

She shook back and forth, then threw him to the ground. The male staggered on his feet, blood oozing from the injury in his neck. She roared again, her claws slashed at the air between them. In another moment she would be on him again, and this time would not let go until he was dead.

The male turned and ran. He opened his wings and took off with a powerful down stroke. He flew as fast as he could as if his life depended on it, which it really did. If he tried to land anywhere near this territory again the female would not hesitate to rip his throat out.

But for now, she let him go. She did not care if that coward left or not, or even if he lived or died. Her main concern now was the safety of her remaining egg and to keep it alive. She walked back into the cave and reformed her pile of rocks around the one remaining egg, picking them up with her mouth and dropping them in a circular pile around it.

From now on, she needed to stay close to the nest at all times, but she also needed food and couldn't leave for a day at a time to get it. Hunting now would take too long with no guarantee of making a kill. What she needed was an easy supply of food that would also let her stay close to the nest.

She had no choice; she would have to raid the farms of men. It was a habit she'd developed and many times tried to break, but always fallen back to.

Human settlements always had a large number of prey animals to choose from that were easy to kill. But even with such a strong temptation, she was hesitant to go. She stood by the nest. Her eyes moved frantically between her egg and the entrance of the cave. She knew her only option was to steal from the humans again, but she was finding it hard to bring herself to it. The last time she started stealing from them almost got her killed, as did the time before that. Sometimes, the scar left by the arrow in her chest still ached.

At the moment, no other choice existed. She would have to kill the human's livestock. The dragon breathed another stream of flames on the nest. With the rocks bathed in fire, she went to the entrance of her cave, flared her wings and took off, her sights on the village.

Chapter 10

Richard pushed open the door of a workshop. The sign above the door outside read *Brown's Blacksmith.* There were few windows, the room was cast in dark shadows. Soot covered almost everything in fine layers of black dust. Richard saw through a doorway the bright glow of a furnace and he heard the rhythmic clanging of a hammer striking metal against an anvil.

He slammed the door hard behind him. The clanging stopped. A voice called out from the workroom. "I'll be right up there." The was a hiss of steam as the metal was plunged in a barrel of water, soon followed by the grinding of coals as it was shoved back into the furnace.

A well muscles, bald man stepped out of the workroom. His arms were thick and powerful, with veins running along them all the way from wrist to shoulder. A leather apron hung around his neck which was covered in ash and scorch marks. His face and hands were also covered with soot and his thick beard had places where the hair was singed.

The blacksmith, Mr. Brown, rubbed his hands on a dirty rag. "Hello, sir."

"Hello, Mr. Brown." Richard said. "I'm here to pick up my order. It is done, yes?"

"Absolutely." Mr. Brown replied. "Just let me go get it." He stepped back into the workshop and came out with a sword in his hands. The blade was covered in a tanned leather scabbard, and the handle was wrapped in leather straps with gold glittering underneath. The every end of the hilt was adorned with a roaring lion's head. "I must say, this is probably my best work to date."

Richard grabbed the word by the hilt and pulled it from the sheath. He held it up before his eyes, the pointed tip aimed at the ceiling. The total length of the sword ran forty inches from the tip of the blade to the bottom of the hilt, with thirty-two of those inches being the blade itself. The pommel was just long enough that Richard could grip it with both hands, but also short enough that he could use it one-handed if he chose. “It’s lighter than I thought.”

“That’s because it’s made with such skill.” The blacksmith took a small block of wood and held it up with one hand. “You may test it if you’d like.” He tossed the wooden block up in the air.

Richard gripped the hilt with both hands and swung the sword in an arch. He felt no drag, no resistance at all, but still the blade sliced through the block like it was nothing. It fell to the ground in two pieces.

“The sword is perfectly balanced, and sharp enough to slice dragon scales.” The blacksmith bragged. Richard paused, he inwardly hesitated at the comment. While he knew Mr. Brown most likely meant it as just an expression, the idea still festered in his mind. Mr. Brown picked up the two halves of the wood block and placed them back together. The seem were they separated all but disappeared. “It is the highest quality I have ever made.”

“That’s good. I’d expect nothing less.” Richard sheathed the sword. He produced a small bag of gold coins from inside his coat and handed it to the blacksmith. “I paid the first half in advance, so here is the second half.” He then took a few extra coins from his side purse and placed them in Mr. Brown’s rough, callused hands. “and a little something extra.”

“Thank you, sir. You are too kind.”

The Last Stand of the Dragon

New sword in hand, Richard stepped back out into the cold. A fierce wind battered him as soon as he stepped outside. Be pulled his wolf-skin coat tighter around his body.

He liked the weapon, it felt right in his hands, but it was actually for Sir Ardose. He walked towards Ardose's manor, the snow crunching beneath his feet. While it was only October, the wind and the snow storms were growing fiercer. In less than two months, winter would set in.

As he came upon the estate his lord lived in, he past the animal pen next to the barn and found five sheep huddled together in the middle of the pen. Richard paused. What were all these animals doing outside? There was no grass for them, an no shelter aside from their own wool. Ardose's servants wouldn't be so careless to leave his sheep unattended like that, so why were they here?

His gaze shifted from the sheep pen to the clouds above. In the sky, he saw a dark ripple move against the white clouds. Small at first, but it grew steadily larger as it came closer. Without noticing, Richard had stopped and stood by the sheep pen staring up at the sky. His exposed hands grew numb in the wind, though he hardly noticed. He focused all his attention on the dark shape in the sky.

As it grew larger, it began to take a more definitive shape. The dark wrinkle became wings. Instead of black, it was a pale green, closer to the color of jade rocks. Soon, it was undeniable what the shape was. A large reptile with huge wings and a mouth full of sharp teeth. Richard's blood ran cold. His worst fear confirmed. The dragon had come.

A cry of panic arose from the village. People screamed and ran as the dragon came in full view. It flew over the village, its wings stretched out. The dragon touched down in Sir Ardose's sheep pen, its wings kicked up a blast of snow which pelted Richard in the face. He winced and covered his face with his arm. His legs caught on themselves and he lost his balance, his arms flailed in the air as he fell back.

The woolly animals in the pen bleated in fear. They scurried around in a blind panic, bunched together as they ran. The dragon roared a loud, deafening roar that split the air. It lunged at the sheep, moving with lightning speed, and snapped its jaws closed around a ewe.

The ewe cried out in terror and pain. It's legs kicked frantically as it was lifted from the ground. The dragon shook its head violently from side to side, the sheep's bones cracked and snapped in its mouth. The screams of the ewe suddenly feel silent with a final snapping of the dragon's jaws. It hung limply from the creature's mouth.

Richard crawled onto his knees. He stared up at the massive creature, unable to look away. Even on all fours, the dragon was as tall as a standing bear and longer than a horse and cart. Its wings reached

from one side of the sheep pen to the other with ease.

It snout was as long as one of Richard's legs and it had a crown of six horns protruding from the back of its head and laying over its neck. Blood dripped from the dragon's mouth.

A monster from Hell. That was what he was seeing now, and there was no denying it. This was a beast from the Devil. Richard's heart refused to beat, he was to frightened to move, too frightened to breathe. His hands clenched tightly around the scabbard of the sword.

A shock ran through his body. The sword! The blacksmith said it was sharp enough to slice dragon scales, now was the perfect time to test it. Richard jumped to his feet with the sword in hand. He gripped the hilt and tore it from the sheath, the blade glittered in the sunlight

The dragon's eyes caught the light from the blade. It blinked swiftly and recoiled, the sheep slipped from its jaws and landed with a flump in the snow. Richard jumped the fence and charged at the distracted creature, the sword held firmly in both hands. He swung with all his strength, the blade sliced through the air in an arch around him.

The dragon reared up on its hind legs, the pointed tip slit a tiny sliver across its chest and a droplet of blood oozed out. The dragon stared hatefully down at Richard, a deep rumbling growl echoed in its throat.

With a swing of its front paw, the dragon caught Richard by the shoulder and sent him spiraling to the ground. The talons, each as thick and strong as meat hooks, tore into his skin and ripped away at his flesh. A jolt of pain shot through his body, the sword flew from his hands, and he landed face first in the snow.

The dragon pulled it claws from his body and stepped away from him. It grabbed the lifeless body of the ewe, flared its wings, and pushed off from the ground. It lifted back up into the air, leaving Richard's body motionless in the snow.

Chapter 11

Richard lay unmoving on the ground. The pearl white snow around him slowly turned red as blood flowed from the open wound. The villagers watched from a distance as the dragon flew away. Once it was gone, a crowd gathered around the sheep pen. Soft whispers and murmurs emanated from the people.

"Richard!" A voice cried out from the crowd. People moved and stepped aside as Rachel forced her way through. She emerged from the gathering and saw Richard's motionless form. "Oh, my… Lord, please, no."

She climbed over the fence, raced to his side, and knelt down in the snow beside him. Her hands trembled before her eyes as she held them over his back. She feared to touch him, afraid he might already by dead, but she still placed her hands gently on his back. "Richard?" Her voice was low and tender. "Please, say something."

A muffled groan escaped his lips. "Have got to… send a rider. Need to… tell… Ardose." Richard squirmed, he tried to push himself up, but his hand slipped and he fell back to the snow. A gasp arose from the crowd as he fell again.

"Don't try to move. You've been badly hurt." Rachel said. "Someone! I need help!" She shouted to the gathered villagers. "We have to get him to the healer!"

"He has been tainted with the poison of the Devil." The priest emerged from the crowd. He was dressed in long, brown robes which reached to his feet and covered his hands. A large, gold cross dangled around his neck. The top of his head was shaven clean, and he walked with a hunch. "The dragon is a beast from the depths of Hell, a servant of the Devil, himself. The very skin of such a monster is tainted with evil, and now that evil is in his veins. He must be brought to the church and beg for God's grace and forgiveness."

"He'll die if we don't get him to the healer first!" Tears flowed down Rachel's face. "Father Josef, please! If we can save his life first, then we can save his soul."

The priest gave a small nod. “Very well. Men, help the lady. Take the boy to Helga.”

Two men climbed over the fence and took Richard carefully in their arms. They carried him as gently as they could; blood still flowed down his arm and into the snow, leaving a trail of red behind. Rachel walked beside them the whole way, tears still falling from her eyes.

They came to the home of Helga, the master of medicine and healer of the village. Rachel threw the door open as the men carried Richard’s limp body inside.

Helga, an old and very heavy woman, sat in a rocking chair by the fire with a pair of crochet needles and a basket of yarn beside her. “What is it you want?” She groaned.

“Helga, it’s Richard!” Rachel said. “He’s badly hurt. There was a dragon! It attacked Sir Ardose’s sheep and he tried to stop it, but it gouged him with its claws and now he’s bleeding to death!”

The clinking of Helga’s crochet needles stopped. She set them down in the basket beside her and stood up, the chair groaning as the weight lifted off it. “Let me have a look at him.”

She pulled the ragged remains of his coat aside and looked at the gashes in his shoulder. “Set him up in the guest room, lay him down with the wound facing up.” She ordered. As the men did so, she took Rachel aside. “I’ll need your help with this. I can’t move as fast as I used to anymore. Are you willing, child?”

"Of course, I'll do anything." Rachel said without hesitation.

"Good." Helga gave Rachel her instruction. "Take that pot, the one hanging above the fire. Do be careful to grab a rag or something before trying to lift it. I need that filled with water and placed back over the fire."

Rachel did as she was told, filling the pot with snow from outside before hanging it back on the hook over the glowing embers and burning wood.

"Once all that melts and begins to boil, take all the cleans towels and rags I have in and put them in the water. We'll need that to cleanse the wounds." The old woman instructed. "Feed the fire, while you're at it. I do believe it is getting cold in here again."

The snow in the pot melted quickly over the fire, and soon it began to boil. With all the rags soaked in the warm water, Helga gave Rachel more instructions. "Now, take that pot again and bring it into the guest room. Oh, before you do that, take that cautery iron there and set it in the coals. We'll need that shortly."

The iron was a long shaft of metal like a fire pit poker, but with a flat metal plate at the end instead of a point. Rachel new exactly what it was going to be used for, she'd seen branding done on cattle and horses. She stuck in into the red hot coals, and then wrapped her hands with a towel to grab the handle of the pot.

She and Helga moved into the room where Richard was being

kept. His left arm was a net of blood from shoulder to fingertips. Helga had Rachel take Richard's shirt off, and then taking the towels gingerly from the hot water, dabbed them on the gash in his back. Richard tensed and squirmed, but the two men that carried him in held him down while Helga cleaned the wound. By the time she was done cleaning it, all the towels had been soaked through with blood. "Now, Rachel, could you bring me the iron?"

Rachel did as she was asked. She took the metal shaft, the end of which now glowed red, and placed the cool end in Helga's outstretched hand. With little warning or consideration, the healer pressed the red hot metal plate against Richard's wound.

Richard bit down on the pillow and cried out in pain. He tensed and tried to pull away, but those holding him in place were too strong. The pain was unimaginable, the smell of burning flesh was unbearable. Once the plate was pulled away, Richard lost consciousness and collapsed on the bed.

Helga looked down at her handy work. The skin around the burn was red and raw, but it would heal in time. The important thing was that the bleeding had stopped. The water in the pot had turned pink from all the blood soaked rags. The healer cooled the cautering iron by dipping it in the bloody water, where it hissed and sputtered as steam rose off from the hot metal.

"Well, gentlemen and lady," Helga said, "I must now ask you to leave. He requires his rest now, and that is best done when no one unnecessary is around."

"Will he be alright?" Rachel asked.

Helga nodded. "He'll be fine. He just needs time to heal and recover his strength."

A low whisper came from Richard as he lay in bed. Rachel and Helga stopped instantly, waiting for him to speak again. "Jade." He moaned. "Dragon."

"Jade dragon?" Helga asked. "What do you suppose that means?"

Rachel shook her head. "I don't know. The dragon that attacked had a sort of pale green color to it."

"Hm." Helga thought. "Jade, the dragon."

Chapter 12

High above the village, the dragon, now called Jade although she did not care, pushed her powerful wings up and down through the air. The lifeless body of the ewe dangled limply from her mouth. Stolen from humans. As she flew over the entrance of her cave, she dropped the sheep to the ground where it landed with a flop in the snow.

A part of her hated herself for this. Having to steal from humans to survive. It was disgraceful. She was supposed to be the most powerful creature on the planet. Her ancestors once hunted the great mammoth caravans across Europe and Siberia, now she could barely survive by stealing livestock.

Jade descended to the ground. She banked her wings and landed softly, her feet sank into the snow and her wings folded tight against her body.

Just as she picked up the sheep in her jaws and carried it inside. She brought it all the way down to her rock nest. Smoke rose from the smoldering remains of the coals. She dropped the sheep and breathed another short stream of fire on the nest. Then she set the wool of the sheep ablaze. As the wool burned away, she snapped at the lightly charred flesh and tore small chunks away with her claws.

A small squeak came from the nest. Jade froze in place. She didn't move, didn't breath, didn't blink. She just waited and listened. Part of her thought she might have imagined it, a hopeful wish that this egg had not died like the other.

Another chirp emanated from the nest, and soon another. Jade dropped the sheep and moved over to the pile of smoldering rocks. She pawed at the stones to dislodge them and reveal the egg. A tiny crack appeared in the shell. The quiet chirps came from the within as the crack grew thicker and longer; the baby inside struggling for freedom.

Jade rolled the egg out of the nest and watched it intently. The still burning carcass of the sheep lay forgotten off to the side. The egg wobbled and shook as the small shell pieces fell away. A tiny snout pushed its way out.

Jade waited eagerly as her baby slowly clawed its way out of the egg. It took over an hour for the hatchling to free itself from the broken shell of its egg. It slid onto the ground still covered in the embryonic fluid. Jade moved in over her hatchling and licked across the baby's face, then over the rest of its body to clean it off. It squirmed and wriggled under its mother's tongue.

The hatchling stood up for the first time, its wide eyes blinked furiously as it took in its first sights. It chirped at its mother, who growled in response.

Jade nuzzled her snout against the hatchling. It was a female, and tiny compared to the mother. Its head barely reached up to Jade's knee. Its horns were only small nubs and its wings were tiny.

The baby chirped for food. Fresh out of the egg and already hungry. Jade led it over to the sheep carcass and tore a small piece of flesh away. The hatchling snapped it up eagerly and had it swallowed in three huge bites. It went back for more food, trying to claw and bite another piece off, but failing to do so. Jade tore another small chunk away and gave it to the hatchling. They continued to feed in this way until the baby was full. It curled up next to its mother and quickly fell asleep.

Jade lay with the hatchling nestled up next to her. She set her wing over the baby like an enormous bird. Her heart filled with an animalistic sense of pride. This was her child, her hatchling. Nothing would take her away from this baby, and she would fight, kill, or die to protect it.

***

Richard awoke on a straw mattress with quilts and blankets layered on top of him. He was sweaty, his body felt week and sore. The pressure from the blankets seemed to hold him down.

A patch of sunlight filtered in though the window above his bed. Just as he turned his head to look outside, a lightning strike of pain coursed though his body, starting from the shoulder. The winced and his eyes clamped shut, tears seeped out through the closed lids.

Moving slowly, he reached his right arm across his chest and over his lift shoulder. He felt the skin change from its usual texture to a rough scab along his back. Another wave of pain washed over him and he withdrew his hand.

“I wouldn’t touch it if I were you.” Helga sat in a rocking chair in the corner of the room watching him. It was only after she spoke that Richard noticed her. She had her crochet needles and her basket of yarn. “I am glad to see you’re awake, however. For a while we were afraid you might not live.”

“How long have I been here?” Richard asked.

"This is the third day." Helga said without looking up from her work. "You were asleep for most of it, but you briefly had a fever last night. It broke this morning. It's actually a miracle you're alive at all."

"What do you mean?"

"That hole Jade tore in you was huge. If Rachel hadn't insisted in bringing you here instead of the church, you'd be dead now." Helga explained.

Richard rested his head back down on the pillow. "That's good to know." His brow scrunched and he sat back up. "Who's 'Jade'?"

"That's the name you gave the dragon, of course." Helga said.

"Name? I never gave it a name."

"You did when you were brought here." Helga looped another notch in her yarn. "Granted, you were delirious and asleep, but the name has stuck. Now that's what everyone is calling it."

Richard shook his head. He pressed the palm of his hand against he eyes and gave a heavy sigh. "I don't care what they decide to call it. I just know it has to be destroyed." He kicked the blankets off the best he could and tried to climb out of bed. His legs refused to support him, however, and he fell back onto the mattress.

"Don't try to stand or walk yet, you're still recovering." Helga said. She still didn't move or look up from the needles in her hands. "It's best if you stay in that bed for at least another day."

"What about the dragon? Has it returned?" He asked.

“It has not. We’ve been fortunate so far.”

He sighed. “I have to get up. I have to send a messenger. Sir Ardose needs to know what’s going on.”

“Riders have already been sent out.” The door creaked open and Rachel stepped inside. The sleeves of her tunic were pulled up over her elbows and she carried a wooden bucket full of hot water and towels in both hands. Her normally unruly red hair was tied up in a bun behind her head. She smiled when she saw Richard. “Glad to see you’re feeling better.”

“I’m not feeling great, though.” He said. The corners of his lips perked up when he saw her.

“Rachel’s been helping me care for you while you’ve been resting.” Helga said. “She’s actually a very competent nurse.”

“That’s nice.” Richard groaned.

He grabbed the blankets with his good hand and tried to pull them over himself, but didn’t get them very far. Rachel set the bucket of water down and helped him. “Here. You’re still recovering. You lost a lot of blood.” Once she had him tucked into bed, she took one of the towels from the bucket and used it to dab his face.

Richard felt the warm soft fabric press against his skin. The heat was soothing to the touch. He watched as Rachel doted over him, her face was flush red, no doubt from the exertion of caring for him for past few days. Having her face so close to his own made him feel warm, much warmer than even the layers of blankets and the hot water on his face did.

The more he watched Rachel, the more he thought about the secret he kept, the one Ardose had asked him to keep and the possible connection it had to her missing brother. Richard hadn't gotten to assemble that search party before the dragon came, and now he felt the need to confess.

"Rachel," he said after great hesitation, "there's something I think you should know. I really think the villagers might need to know it too, but I can't tell them yet."

Rachel stopped with her hand pressed against his cheek. "Yes?" She asked. "What is it?"

"The dragon," Richard said, "I knew it was here before it attacked. I've known for a while, since before Sir Ardose left the village."

A look of surprise came across Rachel's face. She pulled away from him, her eyes wide and lips parted. "You knew?"

Richard slowly nodded and shifted his gaze away. "I saw it from a great distance. I immediately went to Sir Ardose and told him about it, but he asked me to keep it a secret."

"Why would he do that?" Helga asked. She still sat in her chair in the corner, but now she placed the crochet needles aside.

"He said it was for the villages best interest not to start a panic." Richard explained. "He thought I might have been hallucinating or saw a mirage in the clouds. That even if it was there, he thought it might go away in a few days."

"But you didn't tell anyone, even in secret?" Rachel asked.

Richard looked back up at her, he stared into her forest-green eyes. "It was on the wishes of the man I serve." He replied. "I should have told you earlier, but I can't go against the wishes of my lord."

"But if you had told someone… if you had told me…" Rachel's eyes snapped fully open as a terrible thought came into her mind. Her brows then furled down and she glared at Richard. "If you had told us, then my brother might still be alive."

"Now what is that supposed to mean?" Helga asked.

"Dennis went into the woods to hunt the day Ardose left the village, which, according to Richard, was after he saw the dragon for the first time." Rachel's tone was harsh and cold. "He hasn't come home from that hunt even now. I think you know."

Richard was not surprised. He let out a heavy sigh and closed his eyes. "I think the dragon may have killed your brother."

"And you didn't think to tell me!?" Her voice suddenly screeched, loud and cracking. "Once I told you he was missing you knew he was dead! And you knew there was a dragon out there that may have killed him, but you didn't tell me!" Tears formed at the corners of her eyes; one peaked over the edge and ran down the length of her cheek.

Helga pushed herself up from the rocker with a creak and a groan.

She folded her hands together in front of her. “My child, it’s best not to blame the hand for the actions of the mind. Sir Ardose gave Richard an order, and Richard is honor bound as the knight’s squire to follow that order.”

“I know that.” The tears now flowed fully down her face. She seemed to cry so easily these days. “But it doesn’t change the fact that my brother is dead. My mother and I depended on him. We may not survive without him.” Rachel wept, her face buried in her arms at the edge of the bed.

Richard’s heart ached for her. Her grief was true and he was partly responsible for it. If he had told someone what he knew, then it was very possible Dennis might still be alive and the dragon dead.

He pulled his hand free of the blankets and pressed it gently on Rachel’s shoulder. “I am sorry.” Richard said. “and I promise I will avenge your brother’s death. I will slay that dragon”

Chapter 13

Sir Ardose stepped through the door of Cain's shop. The room was still low lit with only the single candle to illuminate it. Cain sat behind his desk with his fingers laced together in front of his face. "You're back, I see." His chilling voice called out. "Any news from your sheep?"

"Funny you should ask that." Ardose held up a folded sheet of paper between his thumb and forefinger. "A rider came with a message. It seems the dragon has made itself known. It came down to the village and killed one of my sheep, my actual sheep, and flew off with it."

A wicked smirk slithered across Cain's face. "As I said, we only needed wait." Cain took the paper and read it to himself. "Your squire was injured in the attack, I see. Any feelings about that?"

"None. He was doing his job as the protector of the village in my stead." Ardose replied.

"And you still have no mixed feelings about letting the dragon destroy that village?" Cain folded the paper back up and returned it to Ardose. "From what I read, those people seem to trust you wholeheartedly. And you would let them die?"

"To get what I want, yes I would." Ardose tucked the note away. "They are only peasants, after all."

"Good." Cain said in a slimy tone. "Get everything prepared tonight. We leave first thing in the morning. It's a two day ride back to your village at this time of year. We need to reap the crops while they're ripe, and then torch the field."

***

Richard tossed and turned in his sleep. The pillow was soaked from his sweat. His dreams were strong and terrible. He struggled against them, but could not escape the images that raced through his fever induced mind.

In his dream, the dragon stood over it. It slashed him with its claws and gouged him in the back. Every time he tried to stand up, it slashed him again. And every time it did, the claws stung like new. He heard its roars, felt the heat of its flames. Over and over the dragon killed him, but each time he stood up and grabbed his sword to keep fighting.

Richard's sleep was finally broken when the door to his room creaked open. His eyelids slowly lifted. They felt crusted and heavy, like he'd gotten no sleep at all. He turned to the door and saw Rachel as she stepped inside.

"Richard," she said, "there's trouble in the village."

He groaned a response. "Is it the dragon? Has it come back?"

"No. It's not Jade." Rachel said. "It's Phillip."

"The drunken farmer?" Richard pushed himself up and rested on his elbows. "What is he doing?"

"He's been talking with a few of the others, principally William and Kenneth, about trying to scale the mountain and slay the dragon themselves."

"What!?" Richard almost jumped out of bed, an action that sent another jolt of pain coursing through his body. He clutched his shoulder more fiercely. "Are they really stupid enough to try that?" He said through gritted teeth.

"That or drunk enough." Rachel moved over to his bedside and grasped his hand in hers. "Richard, you have to talk some sense into them. They won't listen to anyone else, not even Abel or Father Josef. Please, try to convince them not to do it."

Richard shoved the blankets off and kicked his legs off the bed. "Help me stand." He said as he placed hiss hand on Rachel's shoulder. She took his arm behind her head and lifted him up. His legs still felt weak and watery, but with her help Richard was able to stand again. "Were are they now?"

"At *The Roaring Lion*." Rachel answered.

"Then take me there."

***

They sat at the same table as usual. Phillip, William, and Kenneth, three local farmers and common patrons of Abel's tavern, *The Roaring Lion*. A jug of foam topped beer rested on the table before each of them. Phillip clutched the handle of his mug tightly. "Listen, boys," he said, "I've dealt with this before. I've had wolves come down to my farm and kill my animals, and I'll tell you right now, once an animal starts going like that it doesn't stop until its dead. We have to kill this thing."

Kenneth fidgeted in his chair. "Are you so sure? Maybe it'll just go away if we ignore it."

"No, it won't." William interjected. "Once it's done with out sheep, the dragon will start coming after our women and children. It'll come after them at night, burn the village down and swallow us one by one!" He slammed his fists heavily against the table, which shook from the force. "It's not an animal, but a monster from the Devil himself, and it must be stopped!"

"But it was huge!" Kenneth's voice cracked with fear. "Bigger than anything I've ever seen before. We can't hope to fight something like that."

Phillip stood up and smashed his fists against the table. "Listen, you coward! It's going to come back, that's a certainty. We're not safe until it's head it mounted on the walls of this very tavern!" He grabbed his beer and downed it in three hearty gulps. After wiping the foam from his lips, he sat back down. "Look, Sir Ardose is still at least a day's ride from here and Richard is in no condition to do anything. It's up to us now."

The tavern door swung wide open. Richard, with one arm draped over Rachel's shoulders, stood in the doorway. Snow flakes danced around him in the wind. The room instantly fell silent as everyone stared at him.

The quiet was broken when Phillip jumped to his feet. "Richard! You're standing again!"

"Yes, I am." Richard staggered into the tavern. He lifted his weight off Rachel and supported himself as best he could "and I'm here to talk to you. I hear you've been making plans."

Phillip slumped back down on the bench. "News travels fast around here. Yes. We're going to slay the dragon ourselves."

"That's suicidal. What weapons are you planning to use? Pitchforks?" Richard scoffed. "I tried with a sword and barely escaped with my life."

"If you'd let us into Sir Ardose's armory then we could get true weapons. Swords, axes, everything we'd need." William retorted.

"You don't have the training to use a sword properly." Richard said. "It'd just be more of a hindrance. Our best option is to wait for Sir Ardose to return and let him deal with the dragon."

"The longer we wait, the more the dragon will keep attacking us. Soon we won't have a village anymore. It must be stopped now." Phillip said.

Richard turned to the bartender behind the counter. "Abel, help me talk some sense into these men."

"I have tried." The large man said. "They don't listen to reason."

"Won't listen? It's all of you who aren't listening!" Phillip shouted and threw his arms up in the air. "We are under siege! A flying, fire-breathing, hell beast has descended on us and has begun killing our livelihood! and all you fools can do is sit around and wait for someone to come rescue us! We need to stand up for ourselves now, because no one else will."

The tavern filled with silence. No one spoke or moved. Richard sighed and shook his head with despair. “Fine.” He said. “I didn’t want to do this, but you’ve left me no choice.” Richard pushed himself away from Rachel and walked slowly, with much pain, over to Phillip’s table.

He propped himself up with one hand on the flat wooden surface. His other hand reached across to his injured shoulder and his face twisted in a grimace. “In the absence of Sir Ardose, all rights and authority pass down to his squire, which is myself. So that means you have to take orders from me if I give them,” He straightened himself up as best he could, “and I am giving you the direct order not to go anywhere near that mountain. Is that understood?”

Phillip frowned. “Yes, sir.” He sat back down in a huff, his arms folded over his chest.

“Good.” Richard said. He turned to address the whole tavern. “That goes for everyone else, too!” He projected. “Until Sir Ardose returns and the dragon problem is dealt with, no one in this village is to venture into that forest or scale that mountain.” Richard then walked back to the door of the tavern and stepped out into the cold.

Chapter 14

Richard didn't make it very far outside before his strength waned. He stumbled and tripped, and almost fell to the ground when Rachel caught him. "Don't worry, I've got you." She said as she slipped his arm over her shoulders again.

With a choke in his throat, Richard placed and hand over his eyes. The tears were coming now, and he needed to make sure she didn't see them. "I'm sorry. I haven't been able to do anything right so far."

"What do you mean?" She asked. They walked together, Rachel supporting most of his weight, back to Helga's house.

“If I’d warned people about the dragon and ignored Ardose’s orders then your brother might still be alive and we’d have been more prepared for its eventual attack.” Richard said with a weak voice. “If I were better with a sword, I might have killed the dragon myself when it finally did attack and the problem would be solved. But none of that happened. I’ve failed. I can‘t even keep peace in the village without having to pull rank.”

“You’re trying to protect us.” Rachel said. “You’ve already shown the qualities of a great knight.” She paused to open the door of Helga’s home. “Come on. Once you’re healed, and back on your feet again, then we can worry about the dragon and Sir Ardose.” She took him inside and helped him back into bed.

As the blankets were pulled up to his chin, Richard asked, “Where’s my sword?”

“The sword?” Rachel scanned around the room, but found nothing. “Oh.” She said as she remembered. “We put it in the other room.”

“Can you get it for me?” Richard said, he reached out from the side of the bed. “I want to hold it again.”

Rachel left the room and stepped out into the hallway. A few minutes later she returned with the sword, back in its leather scabbard. Richard grasped it by the hilt and pulled it beside him. He laid it on the bed next to him, the roaring lion’s head shimmered at the end of the pommel. “I know what to name this sword.”

“What?” Rachel asked.

“Lion’s Fang.” As he whispered this, his eyes closed and he drifted off. Sleep overcame him.

Richard awoke with a start several hours later by the frightening roar of the dragon and the terrified screams of the villagers. He jolted up out of bed and shoved the shutters of the window open. Cold air rushed in from outside.

A flash of green blurred overhead. Richard watched as the dragon circled over the village, its huge wings flapped up and down. Villagers ran into their homes. They locked themselves inside, hoping the dragon wouldn’t come for them.

Richard grabbed the sword next to him and jumped to his feet. A wave of dizziness struck him, he staggered and fell to the floor, landing hard on his injured shoulder. Pain tore through his body. He cried out in agony, “Aargh!”

***

Outside, Jade the dragon soared over the village. Her chest muscles flexed with each down stroke of her massive wings. The humans below her screamed and ran in fear. But Jade had little to no interest in them, she was after their animals. She flew over a farm, a small flock of fenced in sheep took off running as she descended over them.

The sheep sprinted on their spindly legs, but no creature could run faster than a flying dragon. Jade flew in low, her front claws extended out to grab the first sheep she could. Just as she closed in, she heard a distinctive twang that she recognized all too well. She quickly tilted her wings and veered out of the way just as an arrow shot past her. She circled back around and turned to face her would be attacker.

***

Richard lowered the bow. He cursed silently under his breath, a grimace of pain on his face. His shoulder muscles were still too stiff to pull the bowstring all the way back, so the arrow was fired at half strength. And at the last moment his injury flared up again and he winced, which caused him to miss.

The dragon flew back around and came towards him. The piercing yellow eyes of the great reptile caused Richard's heart to skip a beat. That creature, the dragon, hardly seemed to recognize it had almost been killed. It charged him from the sky and unleashed a torrent of fire.

For a second, which felt like an eternity, Richard could only watch in awe and fear as the flames erupted towards him. He had heard of dragon's breathing fire, but had never witnessed it for himself until this moment. Now that he saw it, the only thought that came to mind was the fires of Hell. This beast was clearly a servant of the Devil.

Richard snapped out of his trance and threw himself to the ground. He curled up with his legs tucked under his body and hands clasped over his head. As he fell face first in the snow, the flames rushed by overhead. He felt the heat on his back and heard the roar of fire as it scorched the air.

***

Jade closed her mouth and the fire ceased. She flew past the human without much thought. He was of little consequence to her now, her target was still the sheep. She dove over the flock, still panicking in their pen, and clutched one in her front talons. It bleated and screamed, kicked and thrashed, all in a vain attempt to escape. While still flying, Jade tossed it in the air and caught it in her mouth. There was a sickening crunch, and the screaming sheep fell silent.

With one in her mouth already, she turned back to the pen and lunged at a second sheep. This time, she brought her whole weight to bare on the smaller animal, crushing it against the ground.

With her prey caught, Jade reopened her wings and thrust them down. A cloud of powdered snow kicked up around her as she slowly ascended into the air. She tilted her wings and pushed herself forward, flying off with her kill.

***

As the wing beats faded off, Richard lifted himself from the snow and watched as the dragon flew away. It had taken two sheep this time, one in its mouth and another carried in its claws. He balled his fists and punched at the ground in frustration. “Grah!” He shouted.

A crunching of snow alerted him to the approach of the three farmers; Phillip, William, and Kenneth. Richard pushed himself up and brushed the snow off his body. He only glanced back to meet their gaze occasionally. “Do you have something to say?”

“You are no substitute for our lord.” Phillip said in a harsh tone. “Sir Ardose would have dealt with this problem long ago. Instead all you’ve done is ineffectually play hero.” He folded his arms over his chest and furled his brows. “You’re no dragon slayer, and you’re no knight.”

“And you think you are?” Richard retorted. “I am a squire, a knight in training, and I’m doing my very best to protect this village. And since you’ve obviously come here to gloat at my most recent failure, just let me say one thing.” Richard spun around with incredible speed and grasped Phillip by the throat. The farmer’s eyes shot wide open and his hands reached up to his neck, gripping and clawing at Richard’s fingers. “I am in charge until our lord returns. That means you are still under my orders and you are still forbidden from ascending that mountain. Now, have I made myself clear yet, or do you need a better reminder?"

Phillip coughed and sputtered. His breath grew short and vision blurred. He managed to vomit up a quiet and strained, "No," for which Richard released his hold. Phillip pulled away, his hand rubbed the soreness around his neck, and he gasped for air.

"Good. Now go home." The three farmers retreated, but Richard was already regretting what he did. He just attacked a man, almost choked the life out of him, all for saying a few words he didn't like. What kind of person would do that? What kind of person was he turning in to?

***

Jade struggled to stay aloft. He journey back to the cave was longer and more difficult than the previous one. This was partially due to having two prey animals with her instead of only one, but more than that was the fire she used to fend off that human attacker of hers. The more fire she used, the harder it was to fly. If she used it all, then she'd be stuck on the ground until her supply replenished.

It was the same human who attacked her with the sword the first time she stole from that village. Usually, humans had little distinctiveness one from the next and she cared not how they looked, but she always took special care to remember those that attempt to harm her.

Why was this one so interested in her? She had no desire to harm him, so did he attack her twice now? She even made sure to take prey from a different field than before so as to avoid him, but he was still there. She thought temporarily of leaving again like she had from her last home, but that was out of the question now with another mouth to feed.

As she flew over the cave entrance, she dropped both seep from her mouth and claws. They landed with a thump in the snow. Once they hit the ground, Jade let out a bellowing roar to signal her return. A chirping growl echoed in response from the cave.

The hatchling scampered out of the cavern to greet its mother. It nuzzled up against Jade's foreleg as once she landed. Its large eyes gazed up at her and it squeaked for food. Although only a few days old, it was already growing quickly.

This was the reason Jade had taken two sheep instead of only one like before. While her chick couldn't eat a whole animal by itself at once, it did need food more frequently than its mother and Jade did not have the energy or desire to make constant trips down the mountain.

The chick latched its jaws around the leg of one of the sheep and started trying to pull it into the cave. It drug the carcass a few feet before giving up and chirping for its mother. Jade grabbed the limp animal and carried it inside. She did the same to the other as well. Once inside, she breathed a small jet of flames across the wool of the animal. In doing so, Jade was instructing her daughter.

Animal fur and wool could not be digested. If she ate it, the hair would clog up her internal organs and possibly kill her over an extended period of time. So, to circumvent this, dragon's simply burned the fur away. This was an important lesson for the young hatchling that fire was not just a weapon but also a tool.

As the wool burned away, Jade tore a small chunk from the carcass and held it out for her hatchling to take. The chick snatched the meet from its mother's mouth and shook it violently. Its teeth were still too small to tear meat with any efficiency, but the hatchling slowly worked it into smaller, more manageable pieces to swallow.

Jade watched her baby with animal pride. Only a few days old, and already the chick had the will of a hunter. In a few years the hatchling would be large enough to start joining Jade on hunts and helping catch its own prey, but for now it needed to rely on its mother. She tore another piece from the sheep and gulped it down. Slowly, helping her daughter along, the two of hem consumed the carcass.

The hatchling also needed to eat furiously because its first hibernation would start soon. In only a matter of weeks, the dragons would enter a state of suspended animation and sleep for three and a half months, awaking some time in early spring. They needed all the food they could get while they could get it, and also to expend as little energy as possible the rest of the time.

Once they fully devoured one of the sheep, Jade stepped back out of the cave and into the sun. The chick followed closely behind. They rested together in the light, the hatchling nuzzled up next to its mother, Jade's wings spread out on the ground to soak up the warmth of the sun. They slept like this for a long time, warm and content.

Chapter 15

Vince stared up that the sky intently. The dreary gray clouds choked off the sunlight. A fierce wing blew in from the north, bringing hail and snow down upon him. A thick black cloak hung from his shoulders and flapped violently in the wind. He gripped his crossbow with both hands, the bowstring locked and a bolt set in place.

In the sky, dark against the clouds, flew a dragon. He recognized it as a male based on its bright orange and red scales, along with its smaller size. The dragon circled overhead, one of Vince's bolts already embedded in its flank.

He kept his eye on the dragon, never letting it out of his sight, even for an instant. If he did so, it would be gone for good. Vince lifted the crossbow up to eye level and took aim down the barrel. The snow swirled all around him, and his hair whipped in front of his face, all obscuring his vision.

His eyes strained, his pulse quickened. The male dragon swooped low and banked, keeping itself just out of range of his crossbow. What he needed was an opening, and he knew the way to get it.

Vince pulled the trigger on the crossbow, the bowstring snapped forward and the bolt flew towards the dragon overhead. As the bolt closed in on its target, the dragon suddenly twisted and rolled in midair out of its path. The bolt flew harmlessly past.

Vince swore silently under his breath. He clicked the lever under the stock forward and the bowstring reset. As he reloaded the crossbow, the dragon folded its wings and dove straight for him.

This was the moment Vince was waiting for. With his crossbow in one hand, he grabbed the cape fluttering behind him and pulled it over himself. Just as the dragon passed over him, it opened its maw and unleashed a torrent of flames upon him. In that split second before, Vince fired his crossbow at point blank range and then pulled the cloak over his body. He was engulfed in flames, but his specially made cape absorbed the heat and block the fire, shielding him from the dragon's inferno.

The bolt struck the dragon at the shoulder, right where its body connected to its wing. The dragon bellowed in pain as the metal tip cut through its scales and embedded in its flesh. The great creature tried to flap its wings, but a burst of pain tore from the wing. It struggled in flight, eventually loosing, and crashed to the earth in a cloud of freshly fallen powdered snow.

Vince lifted the cloak over his eyes so he could see. The snow settled back as the dragon emerged. It fixed its hateful gaze on the mercenary, snarling and growling. Blood slowly oozed out from the injury to its wing, but the dragon hardly seemed to notice. All its focus was on the human that grounded it.

The dragon inhaled deeply, its chest expanded and it reared up on its hind legs. Vince knew exactly what was coming, he was counting on it. He pulled his cape back over himself just as the dragon unleashed all the fire it could muster. Now that it was grounded and without the need to use its internal fuel for flight, it held nothing back.

Vince became surrounded in flame, the roar of the fire deafened him, and the heat was almost unbearable. Beads of sweat formed on his forehead, and the tips of his beard started to singe, but he held firm.

The fire ceased. The heat dissipated quickly in the cold air. Vince threw the cloak off and stood triumphantly. The dragon gasped for breath, steam rose from its mouth. It had put everything it had into that blast, and yet Vince still stood. It inhaled again, but this time only tiny blue flames escaped passed its teeth. All its internal heat had been used it, it had nothing left to burn.

The dragon curled its lips. It roared at its attacker, yet he did not flinch. Vince knew dragon behavior better than most, he could tell this was a sign of desperation. The dragon could not fly, nor could it breathe fire. Now was the time to strike the killing blow.

Vince set his crossbow aside and drew his sword from the scabbard at his hip. Gripping the pommel tightly, he charged the dragon.

Seeing the human come charging at it left the dragon unnerved. It reared back on its hind legs, holding its wings to steady itself, and slashed its claws at the attacker. Vince ducked down under the swinging talons and thrust his sword forward. The blade stabbed dragon flesh, pierced through the tough scales and penetrated deep into the chest and heart. Blood sprayed from wound and splashed across Vince's face and hands.

The dragon roared in agony. Its legs were unable to support itself. The once mighty beast fell to the earth with a thundering crash that shook the ground. It breathed its last just as its eyes rolled back and it succumbed to death.

Vince stood over his kill. His sword was coated with the creature's blood, along with his face and his hands. He panted for air, his chest heaved. He brushed a strand of blood soaked hair out of his face. Then he gripped his sword again, raised it over his head, and brought it back down on the dragon's neck. He hacked at it vehemently until the final strips of flesh were cut and the severed head rolled away from the rest of the body.

With that done, Vince cleaned his sword in the snow before drying it with his cape and sheathing it. He picked up the dragon's head, which was itself larger than a horse's head, and carried it back to where his apprentice, Rennec, waited with the two horses. Along the way he also picked up his crossbow whence he put it.

"Was it the one, sir?" Rennec asked. "The one that escaped in Italy?"

"That it was." Vince threw the severed head into the cart attached to Rennec's horse before climbing on the back of his own. He fit his feet through the stirrups and took the reins. "Now, let us continue."

"Where are we to go, sir?" Rennec asked. He kicked the gelding and it started forward.

"We'll continue east. That female from the Alps is still out there, and it was this direction she traveled." Vince ran his fingers across the scar that ran down the entire right side of his face, from his forehead to his chin. "I know of a village were we can stay."

"How far have we traveled, sir?" Rennec asked.

"These are no longer the mountains of the Alps." Vince replied. "Now, these are the Carpathians."

Chapter 16

Richard sat up on the edge of the straw mattress. His right hand clasped over his left shoulder, rubbing the tenseness and aches out of it. It was getting better now, he could roll his arm all the way around without a problem, and when he tried, he could pull a bow sting back to its full draw length. Still, he was not fully recovered yet.

A knock came to his door. He quickly stood and threw a tunic on before answering. Rachel stood on the other side. "Richard," she said, "Sir Ardose has returned."

"He has?" Richard's voice betrayed his excitement. He rushed over to the door and pushed past her. He found Sir Ardose standing by the fireplace, dressed in a long black cloak with a jeweled headband around his forehead and matching gloves on each hand. He stroked his beard and listened as Helga recounted the recent events, when he noticed his squire. “My lord.” Richard dropped to one knee and bowed his head in respect.

“Richard,” Ardose said, “I read about your incident with the dragon in the letter your rider sent. And have just been told about your brave attempts to slay the beast yourself. I’m glad to see you’re doing well.”

“Yes, sir. Recovering well.” Richard answered, he quickly stood.

Ardose stepped aside; he hung his cloak on the rack by the door. “Allow me to introduce the man who will solve this dragon infestation for us.” He gestured to the old, grim-looking figure. Richard had been so exhilarated in Sir Ardose’s return; he had not noticed the other man standing in the corner, hidden in shadow. “This is Cain; he’s a professional dragon slayer. The moment I heard about what had happened, I contacted and hired him.”

Richard eyes the old man. He was at first confused when this man appeared with Ardose at the door, but now hearing what he was, Richard felt even more concerned. This man looked far too old and frail to hunt dragons for a living, unless it was something he used to do long ago when he was a young man. Still, the young squire gave a bow. “It is an honor to make your acquaintance.”

“I feel the same way.” Cain spoke. Hearing his voice for the first time sent a shiver running down Richard’s spine. This combined with his jutting cheekbones, deeply furled brows, and ice-blue eyes, gave Cain the appearance of a deadly menace. “You lord has spoken highly of you since we’ve met.”

“I am flattered.” Richard said. He kept his lips firmly sealed, concealing his emotions.

“I’d like to remind you, Ardose,” Cain turned back to the knight, “that I have a charge a significant fee for the dragon’s disposal. Every family in the village must produce a small sum for my services.”

“Yes, of course. I have not forgotten.” Ardose waved his hand in the air as if it meant nothing to him.

Richard, however, was shocked to hear this. “Excuse me, my lord,” He said, “A small sum? How much is a small sum? Many of these people do not have much to live on, especially with winter soon approaching. Is this really necessary?”

“I’m afraid it is.” Ardose replied. He gently placed a hand over his squire’s shoulder, and when Richard tensed up from pain, he pulled it back. “I’m sorry. Helga just told me about what the dragon had done to you, but I’d forgotten already. The truth is, we need a man like Cain to deal with this. Once the dragon is dealt with, then life can return to normal, and it is better that the people only have to pay a little coin then have their homes destroyed."

"Sir Ardose, you still haven't answered me. How much is a small sum?" Richard asked again, more earnestly.

"That will be decided tomorrow." Ardose said. "Right now, I want you to go back home and get a good night's rest. We leave out first thing in the morning once the fee has been collected."

"You mean to say I will be accompanying you?"

"Of course. You are my squire, I can't go into battle without you at my side." Ardose said with a smile.

As nice as his lord's words were, Richard still couldn't shake the feeling of danger that emanated from Cain. Nor the idea of the people's coin being taken so casually by this man. Still, he trusted the wisdom of Sir Ardose, and made no fuss about it.

The next morning, Richard found himself standing outside the steeple of the church once again. This time he was dressed fully in his armor with the sword, Lion's Fang, attached to the belt at his waist. He wore a large cloak of animal fur which reached down from his shoulders to his ankles for warmth. He held the reins of three horses, one for each of them, as he waited for Ardose and Cain to finish collecting the dragon slayer's fee.

Looking up at the mountain, he saw dark clouds circling around it. There was likely a storm coming, he thought it might be a better idea to postpone the assault until a better day, but Cain insisted on this day.

The priest, Father Josef, came outside to greet him. “Good morning, my child.” The priest spoke. “I’ve heard our dear lord returned last night. And brought us a savior in our time of need.”

“I’m not entirely sure about that.” Richard replied. With his eyes fixed on the clouds moving in on the mountain, he brought himself to ask, “Father, do you think believe this quest is true?”

“How do you mean, son?” Father Josef asked.

“I have no doubts about slaying the beast, but I’m more concerned about the company.” Richard explained. “Something about this dragon slayer seems frightening to me.”

“You’re still having trouble, then, in trusting in the decisions of your lord.” Father Josef said. “Our Sir Ardose is a man of God, I have no question about that. Whatever he’s chosen to do is the right thing.”

“I want to believe it.” Richard muttered under his breath.

Sir Ardose and Cain appeared from the village and approached the church. The knight held two large leather sacks of gold coins, one in each hand. “Richard!” Ardose called. “Take these and secure them to my horse.”

Richard took the gold from the knight, the weight surprised him and almost made him fall. “Sir, how much is in here?”

“Enough.” Sir Ardose responded. He placed his foot in the stirrup and mounted his horse.

“This feels like the worth of the entire village.” Richard said as he attached the bags of gold coins to Ardose’s saddle.

Cain gave a slight, but sinister grin. “It is. As I said, my services do not come cheap.” Cain saddled his own horse. He grasped the reins tightly in his long, knobby, bony fingers.

Richard stared dumbstruck at the bags of gold he’d just attached to Ardose’s horse. The whole village, every single piece of gold, almost everything they had aside from the clothes on their backs, all right in front of him. And all of it going to this dragon slayer.

He looked up at Sir Ardose, hoping that what was happening wasn’t right. He wished that what Cain just said was not the truth, and that he wasn’t really taking everything they owned. He didn’t get that, instead Sir Ardose simple responded, “I know it seems harsh, now, but you must trust me. It’s for the best.”

Richard took the reins of his own horse and mounted it. He did not look at Cain, or Sir Ardose, or even Father Josef. What had just happened disturbed him greatly, and left his faith in the knight and his lord severely shaken.

“Now, say a prayer for us, Father.” Sir Ardose motioned to the priest. He then snapped the reins and set off for the mountain.

Chapter 17

In her cave nestled within the mountain, Jade gnawed on a stump of bone. Her daughter and her had consumed the second sheep easily and it was time to hunt again. The chick rubbed its face against her and chirped for food.

Jade was torn. She knew that the baby needed food if it was to survive its first hibernation through winter, and in order to do that she would have to pilfer from the village again. But she also knew that to continue stealing from the humans was dangerous, as it had been for her before. As it stood, however, there was no other food source.

She took the bone in her jaws and snapped it in two. The shattered pieces of bone fell to the ground, were the hatchling promptly pounced on them hungrily. It licked at the marrow in the bones with its long tongue. Jade walked to the edge of her cave, a fierce wind howled and chunks of frozen water plummeted from the dark clouds above. Every instinct she had told her to stay in the cave, hunker down, and wait for the storm to pass. All except one. Her maternal instinct pressed her on, told her to brave the storm and go to the village.

Jade gave herself a running start out of the cave. Once she was free of the confining walls, she flared her wings and leapt into the air. The harsh wind battered her and almost forced her back to the ground, but she was strong. She fought the wind and regained her balance in the air. The going was slow, but she was headed back towards the village.

***

Richard's foot sank deep into the snow with each step. First they rode the horses as far up the mountain as they could go, and when the horses had to be left behind they started on foot. The wind was howling around them and snow flew in all directions.

"Are you doing okay, Richard?" Ardose hollered over the howling winds.

"Yes, sir!" Richard called back. He held his hand out in front of his face to ward off the worst of the stinging cold winds. Even so, it chilled him to the bones.

At his waist, sheathed in its leather scabbard, hung the sword Lion's Fang. He tried to give it back to Ardose the day before, but the knight refused. "You used that blade to strike the dragon. You should keep it." Sir Ardose had said. "and besides, after handling it, I prefer my old sword anyway."

Richard had no intention of having to use his sword, the likelihood of him having to face the dragon himself was slim; that was the job of Sir Ardose and Cain, but the possibility still prompted him to carry it. Besides, he didn't trust Cain.

The going on foot was slow, not helped by the hampering storm. Why they didn't choose another day to make this assault on the dragon's cave was a mystery to him. But he carried on, following his lord. The thought of all that gold, the sum wealth of everyone in the village, being given away to this dragon slayer still troubled Richard. Was that what most dragon slayers charge? Was Cain some kind of especially expensive one? Or was there something else behind this? And if there was, wouldn't Ardose know about it?

His thoughts were interrupted when a massive shadow passed over him. He stopped in his tracks and looked skyward. Thick draggles of ash gray clouds filled the air and blocked most of the sunlight, yet he still thought he saw the shadow of something large fly overhead.

Richard immediately thought of the dragon. Jade is what everyone called it, they said he named it in his fever induced sleep, but he cared little if it had a name or not. If the dragon had just flown overhead, then that would mean it was headed back to the village. He needed to warn Sir Ardose. With extra determination, he picked up his stride and moved faster up the mountain after the knight.

“Sir Ardose, my lord!” Richard shouted over the howling winds. “There’s something I must tell you!”

The knight turned around to address his squire. “Later, boy. Look.” He pointed just a little further up the mountain slopes. “Do you see it?”

Richard followed his line of sight and saw a place where the bleak white snow fell away to reveal a dark cavern in the mountain side. “The dragon’s lair?”

“Exactly. Come along.” Ardose patted Richard on the back and hiked up towards the cave. Cain was already waiting for them by the entrance.

“You took too long. You are both young, you should not be beaten so easily by an old man.” Cain produced an unlit torch from his shoulder bag. The old man took a piece of flint and struck against the edge of his sword. A spark leapt off and ignited the end of the torch. “Come on, we have a job to do.” With the burning torch in one hand, Cain lead the descent into the darkness.

Sir Ardose drew his sword and followed the dragon slayer. Richard, however, hesitated by the cave entrance. This cavern was the home of a fire breathing dragon, a servant of the Devil himself. He didn't want to enter, even if it was to slay the beast. "Squire!" Sir Ardose shouted at him from inside the cave. "Come along!"

"Yes, sir." Richard gripped the hilt of his sword tightly and followed his lord inside. It was his duty, along with that of a knight, to kill this monster and send it back to its master in Hell.

A piercing, high pitched shriek came from deeper within the cave. They all froze in place. Richard's hands wrung tighter around the pommel of his sword. He stared off into the deeper darkness of the cave, watching and waiting for whatever had made that scream. The fire from Cain's torch danced and cast its light along the rough rocky walls, which faded to black the further into the cave it went. Richard realized he'd been holding his breath when his lungs started to burn. He let the air out, allowing himself to breathe again.

With his eyes now adjusted to the darkness, he saw a shape move in the inky black void. It moved closer, walking slowly but steadily towards the light. Then it emerged from the dark and they saw it for what it was. Pale green scales, large yellow eyes, a crown of six spiny horns protruding from the back of its skull, and a pair of over-sized wings. A dragon.

A tiny dragon, not much bigger than a dog. It stood no taller than hip height on any of them, and was shorter than the length of a horse.

"Is this all, Richard?" Sir Ardose growled under his breath. His irritation was obvious, as well as his anger. “You were terrified of a tiny creature such as this?”

Richard stuttered in confusion. He was at a loss. The dragon he remembered was an enormous beast of death and destruction, not this tiny, dog-sized lizard.

“Do not be discouraged, sir knight.” Cain said. “This is but a hatchling, less than a few weeks old. It’s obvious that the creature your squire remembers is the mother.”

“The mother?” Sir Ardose asked. There was a hint of relief in his voice. Richard picked up on it, and grew more concerned. Why would his lord be relieved that there was a larger dragon around? “Where is the mother, then?” Ardose asked.

“Perhaps already on her way back to your village. She will return shortly, I presume.” Cain held out the torch to Ardose, who took it from him. “In the mean time, we must still dispose of this.” His long, bony fingers grasped the hilt of his sword, and defying their appearance, pulled the blade smoothly and easily from its sheath. He took up his sword and advanced towards the dragon chick.

***

The hatchling stared with unblinking eyes at the three strange creatures. When it heard them enter it thought its mother had returned already, but instead it found these unusual animals. The chick had never seen anything like them before, and watched them inquisitively. What were they?

One of them, the one with a bald head and scary face, held a burning stick. He gave it to one of the others and then pulled a long, shiny stick from its side and came toward the baby dragon. Fear filled the heart of the hatchling. It didn't like these animals, they frightened it. It growled and snarled as the bald man came towards it, but that didn't stop him.

The man ran at the hatchling and thrust his sword forward. The sharp point of steel easily sliced through the chick's scales and stabbed it through the heart. The tiny dragon screamed in unimaginable pain. Its death rattles echoed off the walls of the cave and out into the raging storm outside. Blood sprayed out from its chest and spilled from its mouth. It never knew why, only felt the agony of death as the bald man pushed harder on the sword It hardly knew life, but now the hatchling knew death.

***

Richard watched in horror and disgust as Cain impaled the dragon chick on his sword. Watching it convulse and twitch, hearing its screams of pain and death, Richard thought he was going to be sick.

He had to turn away and place and hand across his mouth to stop himself from vomiting.

"Richard?" Sir Ardose asked, he placed his hand on the younger man's back. "Are you alright?"

Richard shook his head. He heaved, but managed to prevent himself from puking. He pressed his forehead against the rough stone of the cave wall. It was cold and soothing. What he had just been forced to witness disturbed him greatly.

"Is this your first time watching a dragon slaying?" Cain spoke with sadistic glee. That same horrible smile spread across his face and his eyes emanated an icy cold emptiness. His face was stained with the blood splatter of the dead hatchling. "Trust me, young squire, if you're in the business long enough, you come to enjoy it."

Richard couldn't keep his mouth shut any longer. "You are a terrible, sick man." He spat. "Why Ardose ever chose to hire you is a mystery to me."

Cain's wicked grin turned into a sneer. He lifted up his blood soaked sword. "You have a discipline problem, boy. I think I might have to teach you a lesson."

They were interrupted by the sound of powerful wing beats coming from the cave entrance. Even the howling wind could not compare to the force given off by those wings. Richard's breath was caught in his throat. He knew what that was.

"She's returned." Cain licked the dragon's blood from his lips. "Mommy is going to come looking for her baby."

Chapter 18

Jade landed right at the mouth of the cave. The scent of blood lingered in the air, even in the harsh wind and hail. It emanated from her cave. She hadn't even been halfway to the village when she heard the screams and cries of her daughter carried on the wind, and now she returned to her cave to the smell of blood. Something inside the cave was dead or badly wounded, and she feared as to what it might be.

Hastily, she trotted into the cave. She bellowed a roar, the one to signal her return, but the hatchling did not respond. Inside, now that she was out of the wind, the smell of death was strong. It was accompanied by another scent, the smell of smoke and burning wood. She knew what that was; a torch. Jade continued down her cave. Her heartbeat raced. She knew what awaited her inside.

Three figures appeared out of the darkness, one of which was holding the torch. He was a bearded man brown hair whom she did not recognize. The younger human beside him she knew as her twice attacker from her exploits in the village.

It was the third human who commanded her attention. He was bald with an unsightly face. He held a sword which dripped with blood. At his feet, Jade saw the body of her hatchling laying a pool of its own blood. Its eyes were frozen open in an empty stare of death.

Jade's heart seemed to stop. Al her thoughts ceased, time stood still. Shock, outrage, horror, and terrible grief washed over her in waves. Dead. Her first, and only child was slain.

All of her emotions mixed and turned into white-hot seething rage. A growl rumbled in her throat and her eyes shifted from her daughter to the hatchling's assassin. The bald human with the sword and her daughter's blood still warm on his face. An outrage! The rumble in her throat turned into a roar, the loudest and most powerful she'd ever uttered before. Her jaws clamped shut with a snap that would have shattered bone. Her eyes stared with such intensity they could have incinerated men's souls. Soon, she would incinerate their flesh.

"and now for your plan, Ardose. I believe the dragon is enraged enough." The bald human said.

The bearded human trembled in her presence. "I do believe you're right." He turned to the younger human. "Richard, run!" He threw his torch at Jade. She flinched in shock and swatted at it in the air. Her claws struck the torch and sent it careening aside. In that brief moment, all three of the humans made a run past her and towards the exit.

Two of them managed to get away, the third, the one with blood still on his sword and face, did not. As he ran past her, She threw open her wings and smacked him in the face. He fell to the cave floor, the sword slipped from his hands and he fumbled around looking for it in the dark.

Jade's eyes adjusted quickly to the low light. She found him patting his hands around on the ground stupidly feeling for his weapon. She growled and he stopped moving. While he could not see her, he obviously could hear. He backed away from her, crawling on his hands and knees until he came to the cave wall. He pressed himself up against the rocks, shivering and whimpered in fear. A pathetic creature. First behaving arrogant and proud, now cowering from her like a frightened rat. Jade advanced towards her prey, her foot stomped down on the sword and it shattered under her pressure.

The dragon unleashed an inferno, a huge stream of fire erupted from her jaws like a fiery volcano and engulfed the defenseless human.

His terrible screams echoed through the cave. His clothes burned away, along with his skin and flesh.

Only after his screaming finally ceased did Jade stop. The charred remains of the human lay before her, fire still danced across his burnt form. What little remained was mostly bone, scorched back. An empty skull lay on the floor with its mouth hung open in a silent scream of horror.

In all her anger, Jade had forgotten the other two that escaped her. But she did not care. Her attention turned away from the still burning human corpse to the lifeless remains of her daughter. She pressed her snout against it, nuzzled the baby as she had done before. Already, it had become cold in the mountain cave. Jade let out a sorrowful howl of grief and despair.

***

Richard's legs ached as he sprinted down the mountain slope. Ardose ran ahead of him. Panting and gasping for breath, he felt as if his chest would explode. His heart pumped rapidly in his chest, harder than he ever thought it could.

"Quickly, boy!" Ardose shouted over his shoulder. "To the horses!"

"Sir!" Richard gasped as he ran. "Wait!" Sir Ardose's speed slowed until he came to a full stop. The knight placed his hands on he knees and panted, wisps of vapor from his breath floated up around his face. Richard reached his lord's side and stopped to catch his breath as well. Once he had managed to steady himself, he asked, "What about Cain?"

A terrible scream answered him. It echoed down from the cave above them, accompanied by the roar of fire. Richard found himself frozen in place with terror. He listened for a great while before the terrible sound finally stopped.

"It's over. There's nothing to do for him." Ardose said. "Come on," he turned away and continued down the mountain. "We need to get to the horses."

"You're right." Richard said. His voice trembled more than he thought it would, and he hated himself for it. Try as he might, once again he had failed. "We have to warn the villagers."

"Warn them? No, it's far too late for that." Ardose said. "We need to get away from here as fast as we can. Soon that dragon will return to the village and burn it down. There's no hope for them, anymore."

"What!?" Richard stammered. He raced after Ardose and grabbed the knight by his arm. "No hope? If they're in mortal danger then we have to go back!"

"We can't, boy!" Ardose shouted. He pulled away roughly. "By the time we get there it will already be on fire. Half of it will be ash and the rest in flames. The only thing we can do is get ourselves to safety."

"But they're depending on us! We're supposed to protect them, we cant just abandon them to their fate like this!" Richard's voice grew steadily louder.

Ardose struck his squire across the face, sending Richard sprawling to the ground. "Be quiet! I am your lord and you will address me as such!"

Richard lay on the ground, his hand pressed lightly against the red spot on his face. Never before had Sir Ardose ever lain a hand on him, and certainly not in such a way as this. He choked back a sob in his throat. "My lord," he said as he stood, "I am loyal to you, but I am also loyal to my duty as a squire and future knight of the realm. If those people are in danger, it is my job, and your job, to protect them."

Ardose scoffed at Richard's words. "Future knight? Don't make me laugh. You were never going to be a knight. You're just a lowly peasant born orphan. What you have now is as good as it could ever get for someone like you in this world. Duty. Honor. Titles. None of that every gets you anything, boy. I had hoped you'd come with me."

"What do you mean?" Richard asked.

"This was all a part of the plan." Ardose said. "The fact of the matter is, Richard, that I am tired of this place. Tired of being a knight and having to answer to the peasants of this land." He let out a small chuckle. "I wanted to get away so badly, but if I abandon the village I would be christened a coward and be forced to live with that shame my whole life. Not shame for myself, mind you, but the shame everyone would heap on me. But when you told me about the dragon, I saw my chance."

Richard could hardly believe what he was hearing, but he wanted to know. "Chance for what?"

Ardose continued. "I knew that if the dragon attacked the village and everyone in it died, then I could walk away a free man. I would be assumed dead like the rest of the villagers, possibly even a hero who died valiantly. But before that could happen I would need money, enough gold to live off of comfortably as I reestablished myself as a mercenary sword-for-hire. And for that I would need Cain."

"But, why?"

"Cain was a professional dragon slayer. If I hired him and he charged a fee, then I could split the proceeds from him after we enraged the dragon enough to force it to attack. And now that he's dead, I don't have to share the gold with anyone." Ardose turned away from Richard and gazed back down the mountain side. "I had hoped you'd come with me, I rather fancied you as a squire. But it seems you've made up your mind. I'm leaving now, do what you will."

"Is that why you wanted me to keep it a secret?" Richard asked before Ardose could walk too far. "You didn't want anyone to find out so you'd have enough time? And to force them to pay any price?"

"You catch on well." Ardose said. "Yes. And I had a close call, too.

A hunter boy came up to me on the day I was to leave and also informed me of the dragon. he was even so kind as to lead me to where he saw it. I had to keep him silent, however. A knife in his back was sufficient."

"A hunter boy?" Richard's knew of whom Ardose spoke, and it made his blood boil. "You mean Dennis?" His teeth clenched.

"Was that his name? I keep forgetting. It hardly matters now, anyways."

"It mattered to his family. It mattered to his sister, Rachel!" In a blind fury, Richard fumbled and grasped his sword. He pulled it from the sheath and it glistened in the light. "You murdered him! He trusted you, and you stabbed him in the back!"

"He was only a peasant." Ardose said with disinterest.

This was the last straw for Richard. He shouted a battle cry and charged at the older knight, the sword Lion's Fang in hand. He swung at Ardose's head with all his strength, fully prepared to kill him.

Only Ardose quick reaction saved his life. He drew his own sword and stopped Richard's attack with a quick block. "What do you think you're doing, boy?" Ardose said as he shoved Richard back. "You would dare to attack me? Attack your lord?"

"You're not my lord anymore." Richard hissed through gritted teeth. "You're a murderer, and a coward who would run away and leave the people that trust you to die! You are not the man I swore service to. You are no longer my lord."

"That's unfortunate. You did make a decent squire." He lifted his sword and took a stance. "Make your move then."

Chapter 19

The two of them faced off, Richard gripped Lion's Fang tightly, waiting for Ardose to make the first move. The wind howled around them, capes flapped in the air. Finally, Richard charged at his former master. He pulled his sword back over his shoulder and swung with all his might. Ardose parried the attack with his own sword.

Metal clanked together with a deafening ring. Sparks flew from the blades as they struck. Again and again Richard brought his sword to bare down on the knight, and each time Ardose deflected it. "Come on, boy. I taught you better than this." As Richard moved to attack again, Ardose grabbed him by the arm and yanked him close.

The knight kicked him in the stomach, sending the young man sprawling on the ground. “You’ll have to do better than that.”

Richard did not return his master’s taunts. He got back on his feet, took up his sword, and moved in for another attack. But this time Ardose struck first. The knight swung his sword through the air in an arc right at Richard’s head. He ducked at the last moment and ran with his sword thrusting forward, only to find himself getting a face full of Ardose’s foot.

Richard staggered back, his hand clasped over his nose and blood trickled down his face. He looked at the smears of red on his hands, and in that distracted moment Ardose made another assault. Richard just barely blocked it, but the force of Ardose's attack made him loose balance and he fell to the ground.

Lying on his back, Richard grabbed his sword and tried to stand, but Ardose planed his foot down hard on his wrist. The knight’s other foot stomped on Richard’s chest and forced him back to the ground. “This is it for you.” Ardose raised his sword over his former squire and prepared to deliver a final blow. “And if you’re worried about the villagers, don’t be. They’ll be joining you soon enough.”

Richard had no time to waste. The glittering steel blade of Ardose’s sword was coming down on him. Desperately, he tore up and handful of snow with his free hand and threw it in the knight’s face. Ardose recoiled and grimaced. With that moment of distraction, Richard shoved Ardose back, forcing the knight off him. Richard took Lion's Fang and trust it up, the blade pierced between Ardose's armor plates and into his exposed underarm.

Sir Ardose gasped in pain and shock. Blood poured out onto the snow in great spurts. Richard yanked his sword back and another burst of blood spewed forth. Ardose clasped his hand over the gaping wound, but it did little to slow the bleeding. He fell to his knees, already feeling his life slipping away and the cold engulf him.

Richard stared in abject horror at what he had done. He watched as his former lord stumbled and finally fell face first to the snow. The frozen white snow around him melted and turned red. Ardose's breathing became weak and labored, blood dribbled from his mouth and he coughed and sputtered. Finally, his last breath escaped and he died.

Richard stood. His legs felt terribly weak under him, his stomach pitched and finally he couldn't stop it. He ran to a tree and heaved up everything he had in his stomach, it splattered to the ground in a heaping steaming mess. He pressed his face against the sappy bark of the tree, welcoming the cold roughness on his face.

He'd just killed someone. That thought struck him and stabbed at his heart more than any sword could. Now he was a murderer no better than Ardose of Cain. Slowly, he stepped away from the tree and away from Ardose's body. He didn't want to see it anymore. Not that he would ever be free of it, the image of his sword buried in the knight's flesh was now burned into his mind like a brand.

He took a handful of snow and cleaned his sword. He then dried it with his cape and continued down the mountain. He soon found the horses, still tied up where they had been left. One of them saw him and whinnied, shaking its mane. Richard stroked the horse's face as he slowly untied them. Then, having mounted his horse and leading the other two by the reins, he headed back towards the village.

* * *

"Richard!" Rachel shouted when she saw him riding back to the village. She ran out to greet him, and helped him climb down from his horse. "Are you alright?" She asked. "Where's Sir Ardose and the dragon slayer?"

He let out a heavy sigh. "When we got there," Richard began, "we found the lair empty except for a dragon chick. Cain killed it. And that's when the mother came back. The big dragon, Jade, attacked us. Ardose and I escaped, but Cain didn't make it."

"Oh." Rachel said. She placed her arms around Richard and held him tight. "I'm sorry," and when she pulled away, "and Ardose?"

Richard shut his eyes and winced. His face twisted in resentment. "He's dead, too. I…" he struggled to confess, "I killed him."

Rachel stepped away in shock. her hands hovered over her lips. "You… did what?"

"He told me he planned to leave. Let the dragon burn the village to the ground and run away. He wanted to keep the dragon a secret so much he killed your brother, Rachel." Richard said. "Dennis saw the dragon, encountered it, but it didn't kill him. He told Ardose about it, and then he stabbed him in the back to keep him quiet."

"Richard, I…" Rachel's voice was weak. "I don't believe this."

"And neither do I."

Richard and Rachel turned and saw Phillip approaching. The farmer approached with William, Kenneth, and an entire mob of other angry villagers at his back. Many carried burning torches, others carried pitchforks, smithies hammers, and a few even had homemade bows and arrows. "Whatever you claim, I won't trust it. And neither will the rest of us."

"Phillip, what are you doing?" Richard asked. He looked past him and saw the angry mob of villagers Phillip lead. "Where is everyone going?"

"We're going to do the job that you can't. We're going to slay the dragon ourselves." Phillip said. "And this time, you can't stop us." He turned and looked back over his shoulder. "Isn't that right, everyone?"

The crowd answered in a unified cheer. Richard could hardly believe his eyes. Almost every man in the village had gathered, led on by Phillip's words and prepared to climb the mountain. "Phillip, listen to me," Richard said, "you can't do this. We need to evacuate everyone from the village while we can. The dragon has been enraged and will be coming back. This time she's not just going to steal a few sheep, she's going to kill us all."

"Would you look at that?' Phillip said with a smarmy tone. "Now he wants to evacuate us. He thinks we're just going to bow and obey him like dogs because he's a squire to some dead lord." He suddenly punched Richard hard in the face. Exhausted from his climb up and down the mountain, as well as his fight with Ardose, Richard twisted and landed hard on his side.

"Phillip, what are you doing!?" Rachel cried. She knelt at Richard's side.

"I'm taking matters into my own hands, now. I'm not going to wait for some holier-than-thou squire boy to try and fail to protect us."

Richard rubbed the side of his face, a bruise was starting for form. "Phillip," he said as he stood, "I know we haven't always seen eye to eye, but you have to listen to me now. Sir Ardose didn't want to save any of us, he wanted to leave us to the dragon's mercy. We need to get everyone out of here before it comes back and burns this whole place down."

"Phillip, listen to him, for goodness sake!" Rachel pleaded.

"No!" Phillip struck her with the back of his hand. Rachel cried out in surprise and pain as she fell to the ground.

Richard watched in shock and horror. He'd had enough now. He reached for his sword when suddenly William and Kenneth both tackled him. They grabbed him by the arms and forced him to his knees. Richard struggled, but could not escape their grasp. Phillip stood over him, he had a sadistic grin on hi face as he popped his knuckles. "You know, I've really been looking forward to this."

His fists pounded into Richard's face, each time the young squire winced and moaned. The sounds of the punches rose over the crowd as they watched in silence. Richard wheezed for breath. His face was swollen and bruised, blood dripped down his split lip, his nose bloody, and his eye was black.

As Phillip rubbed his sore knuckles, the glittering gold of the sword hilt at Richard's side caught his eye. "Hmm," he grinned and pulled the sword from its sheath. Richard tried to fight against his captors again, but they held him firm and he was forced to watch helplessly as his sword was stolen. "I don't think you'll be needing this anymore." Phillip said. He held the Lion's fang up in front of his face and stared at its well crafted blade. "Tie him up!" He ordered William and Kenneth, "and lock him inside. I'll finish with him later."

As he was being dragged away, Richard watched as Phillip turned back to the crowd and raise the sword over his head. "Sir Ardose is gone, the dragon slayer has died in defense of our lives, and the squire is a failure! But he was right about one thing, the dragon will return! We're not safe until its head it mounted on a wall!" The crowd cheered and roared with enthusiasm. "I say we rid ourselves of this flying beast! Who's with me?"

"I am!" A voice cried out from the crowd.

"I am!" Came another.

And another, "I am!"

"Good then!" Phillip said. "Bring whatever you can! Axes, hammers, shovels, pitchforks, and light those torches! We'll lay siege to the dragon's cave and bring back its head!"

Just as the mob began its march towards the mountain, Richard was dragged into one of the houses. His hands and feet were bound with ropes and his mouth gagged. He struggled, frantically fought against them, but to no avail. He was then lifted and thrown into a closet, where he landed with a hard thud. William and Kenneth stood right outside the door looking down on him.

"Don't worry," William said, "we'll be back for you."

"And then Phillip will finish you off." Kenneth slid his finger across hit throat for emphasis. Then they slammed the closet shut, leaving Richard alone in the dark.

Chapter 20

Jade slept in her cave next to the cold, lifeless body of her daughter. She had not ventured back to the village as Ardose thought she would, instead deciding to stay in her cave with her hatchling, even with it being dead.

A sense of guilt filled her heart. If she had only been here when the human's came then she might have saved her daughter. In all her life Jade had only been concerned about her own life and well-being, but having a baby changed all that for her. Suddenly she had someone who depended on her for everything, and whether it was just maternal instinct or motherly love, Jade would have sacrificed anything to protect that hatchling. But now it was all moot. The chick was dead, and nothing could change that.

The sound of human voices echoed in from outside and disturbed her sleep. Jade arose and walked to the entrance of her cave, only to find a large number of them all hiking up the mountain towards her. There were dozens, if not hundreds of them. Jade stepped back, recoiled in fear. never before had she seen so many all at once.

"There it is!" The one leading them shouted. He held a weapon that she recognized, the sword of he would-be attacker. But it was a different human this time. "Come on! Fire all arrows!"

There was a twang of bowstrings as the wooden shafts of arrows flew at her. The aim of these humans was not great, as the arrows all missed and merely bounced against the rocks of the cave.

Jade snarled and tried to retreat in fear, but then she stopped herself. It was happening again. Every time she's tried find a home, they would come. No matter where she went, no matter how far she flew, no matter how hard she tried to avoid them or out run them, they were always there. And they always came for her with swords, with axes, with bows and arrows, with torches and pitchforks.

Why? Why did they hate her so much? Why did they want to kill her? She had never harmed a human except in self defense, but they just kept coming.

It was then that she came to a realization. It was never going to stop. They would continue to hunt her to the ends of the earth if need be, and they wouldn't stop until she was dead. They hated her, and they were also afraid of her. They feared her as a monster.

Fine then. If it was a monster they feared, then a monster she would be. Jade stepped back out of her cave. She flared her wings as wide as they could go and reared up on two legs. The dragon let out a blood-chilling roar of rage and hate. The human mob stopped in their tracks, suddenly afraid to face her. Her wings flapped, kicking up a cloud of snow all around her. Soon, she managed to get herself off the ground.

She flew over the humans, flying circles over them as they watched her stupidly. Then, with a tilt of her wings, she flew down in a perfect line over them. Some of them started to run, others fought with themselves for a path of escape, but Jade would give them no escape. She unleashed her fire just as she descended over the mob.

The humans ran in terror. Some of them were doused in flames, screaming and running like feeble animals. Any unified force they once held together was no gone in blind panic. Jade circled back on them for another pass and once again lit them ablaze.

One human, the one with the sword, ran away from the rest as fast as he could go. He ran in blind terror, leaving the fellow human's to their fate. Jade took chase after him. He was the one who brought them here, and she would not let him escape her wrath.

Phillip kicked his legs over the snow as he took off away from the crowd. The cries and screams of pain and terror echoed behind him as the villagers burned in dragon fire. That would not be him, he would get out of here while he still had a chance.

A vicious roar split the air. He barely glanced over his shoulder to see the dragon soaring overhead and right on his tail. Phillip almost wet himself in fear. He ran faster, throwing the sword he stole from Richard aside and letting it fall in the snow forgotten.

He ran out into a clearing without thinking, and the dragon was on him. It swooped down from above like a hawk attacking a frightened rabbit. The dragon reached out with its talons and caught Phillip, the claws dug into his back like enormous meat hooks. He screamed in agony as he was forced down face first into the snow, the dragon's full weight held him down.

Then with three powerful wing beats, the mighty flying reptile lifted into the air again, carrying Phillip in its clutches. He thrashed and struggled in its grasp, but each twist of his body sent another spike of pain through him. He felt his warm blood seep out from the gouges in his back and down his legs. The dragon flew him back over the crowd of burning villagers, pulled its claws back, and dropped him.

Phillip plummeted from to the ground. His arms and legs flailed in the air as he fell, as if he could stop himself somehow. His heart felt like it was in his throat as the ground and burning bodies came closer with each passing second.

He crashed on a burning corpse, his leg bones snapped upon impact. He lay in the fire in excruciating pain as the flames caught on his clothes. Soon, he was engulfed in fire the same as the others.

Jade watched the humans died in fire below her. Those that had managed to get away ran as fast as they could back down the mountain towards their pitiful village.

She was thrilled, exhilarated in fact. For once in her life she was able to strike back against her oppressors, and it felt good. Her thirst for blood and vengeance was not satiated with this, she wanted more. She wanted to see them all suffer, watch them all burn. All of them, everywhere, they would all pay for the death of her daughter.

And she would start with this village. With another angling of her wings, she turned away from the dying mob and headed for the small human settlement at the base of the mountain.

Chapter 21

The room was dark and confined. Richard sat on the closet floor with his back to the wall and his knees pressed up against the door. His hands were bound behind his back and feet tied together at the ankles, a gag wrapped around his mouth.

His face ached all over, and the rest of his body didn't feel much better either. He struggled and pulled on his bindings, but could not escape. He couldn't even stand.

What was the point anyways? If the dragon was coming, what did he care anymore? Even after everything he's done to protect these people, they turned on him, beat him, and left him tied up like this. Why risk his life anymore for people that didn't respect him?

And besides, what if they did succeed where he failed? What if an angry mob did kill the dragon when he could not? There was no reason to fight anymore.

There was a creak from the outside as the lock came undone. The door slowly pulled open, allowing a narrow pillar of light to fall in. The gap grew wider as the person outside pulled it open. Richard's heart began to race. He remembered the threat Phillip gave before they left, and feared they had come back for him. When he saw a hand holding a knife, he thought it was true.

That is until the door opened fully and he saw Rachel standing on the other side. "Richard," she said, "I'm here to save you." She knelt down next to him, set the knife on the floor, and untied the gag on his mouth.

Richard gasped for breath as she pulled the dirty rag away. "Rachel! Am I ever glad to see you." Tears of joy peaked at the corners of his eyes.

She took back up the knife and sawed through the ropes around his ankles. Once they were cut, she helped him stand and cut the ropes around his wrists. She gave a satisfied grunt as the last of the cords snapped and fell away. "There."

Richard spun around and embraced her. And then, without a

second's thought, he kissed her. Only after their lips parted and he saw the startled look on her face did he realize what he'd done. "Oh!" He released her and stepped back, averting his gaze. His face turned red from embarrassment. "I'm sorry."

"For what?" Rachel said, a joyful smile on her face. "I enjoyed it." She stepped over to him and placed her hand in his. Then, looking into his eyes, she graced his lips again with her own.

Richard had never felt so happy in his life. With Rachel in his arms and her soft delicate lips against his, this must be heaven. "Come on," she said after they parted again, "we need to get out of this place."

"Why?" He asked, his mind still in a daze. But as they stepped outside he heard it on the wind, the angry roar of a vicious dragon. He looked up at the mountain with horror, all the color ran from his face. "It's coming back."

"Just like you said it would." Rachel said. "We need to leave, now. You were right, Phillip's mob did nothing except further enrage it. If we don't leave now, we'll die when it burns the village."

Leave? Run? Yes, that sounded nice. Go with Rachel and escape before the dragon came. He still had the gold from Ardose's failed plan, they could use it to build a life somewhere else.

Richard stopped just as he thought of the gold. This sounded exactly like Sir Ardose's plan, and he would have none of it. "No, I can't leave." He said. "I'm the only defense this village has left, it's my job to protect it."

"But, Richard," Rachel pleaded, "you've seen what these people think of you now. They all hate and blame you, why make yourself suffer anymore for their sake?"

Richard clenched his fists. He held his chin high as he glared up at the mountain, anticipation what was to come. "I am a squire, a knight in training. And a knight's duty is to protect the people who serve under him. I'm not running away from this creature now." He turned and raced off towards Sir Ardose's old manor.

"Where are you going?" Rachel cried as she chased after him.

"The Armory!" Richard stated. "I have to prepare!"

***

The church bell rang from its tower as the dragon approached the village. The beats of her wings could be heard while she was still miles away, and her angry roars filled the air. She was not here simply to steal and run again; this was a deliberate attack.

Father Josef ran up and down the streets, knocking on doors and urging people out of their homes. "Come, come, quickly! To the church! Everyone will be safe there!"

The people followed the priest, mostly women and children, and went to the large stone and wood building. The bell rang, villagers crowded inside. Father Josef stood by the tall church doors and hurried people onward. "Are you sure we'll be safe here, Father?" A young woman asked, her baby cried in her arms.

"Yes, of course, my child." Father Josef assured her. "The dragon is a minion of the Devil, and this is the house of the Lord. God's will be done, the dragon cannot harm us here."

The woman ran inside. With no time left to search for refugees, Father Josef pulled the heavy doors shut. They closed with a powerful sound. The priest, along with the few remaining strong men, lifted a heavy beam across the doors to lock them.

Jade began her final descent towards the village. Not everyone had managed to make it to the church in time, and they began to run in fear at her approach.

As she flew over the wood houses, she unleashed a stream of fire upon them. They burst into flames, the wood splintered and cracked from the heat. People screamed in terror. Some were still in their houses when they were set ablaze. A child's terrified wails were heard, people ran from their homes as they burned.

Jade flew back down for a second pass, another torrent of flames erupted from her jaws. This time she aimed not for the structures, but for the panicking people. They were engulfed in flames, their skin melted and flesh burned.

The dragon landed on one of the wooden buildings, its frame

groaned and creaked from her weight. She heard the quiet whimpering and huddled murmurs of the humans hiding inside. She tore the roof apart with a few swipes of her powerful claws, the shingles flew away with each strike. Jade smashed her way inside, finding a woman and two children cowering together in a corner of the house. The children clutched to their mother's side and she held their faces against her body, in a vain attempt to shield them from the dragon.

Jade snorted and hissed. She pulled her head back out of he house and took off into the air. But as she lifted off, she breathed another burst of fire upon the house. The humans inside shrieked in horror as their home burned down around them, trapping them inside and sealing their fate.

She flew over the village again. Smoke rose in great, black plumes as houses and buildings burned. People tried to run, but they had nowhere to go. Jade spotted one human, a tall man with a bald head and thick black beard, as he ran dead on away from the burning village. She swooped down low behind him and caught him in her claws. He cried out in fear as her talons sank into his flesh. She quieted his screams when her jaws snapped closed around his head, the skull crushed like an eggshell.

This was her revenge. The fury of a dragon had been unleashed, and she would not rest until every human in her path was dead.

***

Richard emerged from Ardose's manor, a quiver of arrows strapped across his back and a strung bow in his hands. He'd taken one of Ardose's old swords and belted it to his waist. Outside, he saw the devastation wrought on the village by the dragon. Almost every house he could see was covered in flames, the shrieks and cries of terror and death rose up from the inferno. If there was a Hell, this was it.

A flash of movement above caught his interest. He saw the shape of the dragon in the smoke, her powerful wings fluttered in the wind as she circled overhead for another attack.

He pulled an arrow from the quiver, locked it on the bowstring, and took aim. Just as the dragon swooped in low, he fired. The arrow flew through the air and struck its target, the metal point embedded in the dragon's scaled chest. She roared in annoyance and pain.

The dragon twisted in the air as Richard fired another arrow. This one missed. He notched another into he bowstring and pulled back just as Jade flew down to attack him. He released, but the arrow deflected off one of the dragon's horns.

She dive-bombed him, snapped her jaws at his face and racked her claws for his skin. Richard threw himself to the ground just as the dragon past over, her trail smashed into Ardose's manor and sent splinters of wood flying everywhere.

Jade flew overhead again. While in the air, she reached under her wing with her jaws and yanked the arrow free, snapping it in two. She let it fall back to the ground, forgotten.

Jade turned back towards her attacker and stared him down. It was the same human as before, the one that had been her enemy ever since she came to this mountain. If anyone was to blame for this, it was him. She dove at him with all her might. Just as Richard got back to his feet and took another arrow, Jade swooped down over him. She struck him with her tail. He fell back to the snow, the bow flying from his hands.

Jade banked and landed next to him. As he tried to stand, she placed her front foot on his chest and forced him back down. Her talons scraped against the armor breastplate he wore, and slow cut through the metal. She glared down at him, her lips curled back and she snarled. He looked back up at her with the same fierce stare.

Richard clawed at the dragon's foot, tried to force it away, but the creature was too strong. Even with the armor breastplate on, he could feel the monstrous strength of the beast. She hissed at him, her mouth opened and strings of saliva dripped down from her fangs. She was about to attack, and he knew it.

Out of the corner of his eye, Richard saw someone charging out of the inferno towards him and the dragon. Her bright red, wavy hair bounced behind her as she ran. It was Rachel! She carried the broken half of an arrow in her hand. "Rachel! Stop! What are you doing!?" He shouted, but his voice was drowned out by the roar of the fire.

Rachel ran right up to the dragon and thrust down with the sharp end of the arrow. It dug into Jade's skin, pierced the flesh and drew blood. The dragon screeched in surprise. She jumped away, Rachel tore the arrow back and continued to stab her. "Leave him alone!" Rachel screamed. Each time she jabbed the metal point into the dragon, a jolt of pain scored through Jade's body.

Jade took one swipe at her attacker. The dragon's claws caught the girl and threw her to the ground. Three large diagonal slashes scoured her flesh.

Richard watched in horror. "Rachel! No!" He screamed. He jumped back to his feet and drew the sword at his waist. Just as he was about to charge the dragon, the bell from the church steeple rang again.

Both Richard and the dragon turned as they heard it. The people inside must be ringing it thinking that the sound can drive the dragon away. It had the exact opposite effect. Jade left Richard and Rachel behind and charged for the church.

Chapter 22

Father Josef stood at the podium and looked down at the people gathered in the chapel. Everyone held tightly together, gathered in the center of the church. They could hear the screams outside and saw the fire burning through the stained-glass windows. No one spoke a word, few dared to breathe.

"Everyone," the priest said as he raised his hands, "let us remain calm. This is the house of God, we are safe here."

"It'll come for us!" Someone cried out in terror. "It'll come and kill us!"

"You are mistaken. The forces of evil cannot enter this Holy domain." Father Josef spoke. The ring of the church bell reverberated throughout the chapel. "That ringing is the power of God, and the Almighty will keep his faithful children safe."

Suddenly, the heavy church doors shook. There was a powerful roar from the other side and they shook again. The wooden beam that kept them locked shuttered as the dragon slammed all her weight against the other side. A cry of terror arose from the villagers gathered inside, they ran from the doors, some even jumped over the pews on their way up to the podium where the priest stood.

There was a terrible snarling and raking sound as the dragon drug her claws against the doors. Deep gouges cut through the wood as her talons scratched at the old church doors. Jade grew ever more frustrated as she tore at the front of the church. But try as she might, the doors would not budge. She backed away from them and unleashed a burst of fire. The wood caught ablaze and started to burn.

Inside, the people coward away from the doors. The dragon had stopped trying to force them open, but now they could see and smell the smoke as it drifted in from the cracks. "It's burning!" The frantic woman from before cried out. "It's burning, we're all going to die! It's coming for us!"

"Be silent!" Father Josef raised his voice. He stepped around the people and stood before one of the windows, the one which depicted a valiant knight stabbing a dragon through the heart with a lance. "This image represents evil being struck down by the might of God." He held out his hand to the stained-glass window. "I speak in the name of the Lord, and I'm telling you that no evil will harm us-"

The window shattered behind him as the dragon's head burst through. She roared triumphantly as she crawled inside. A shriek of panic rose from the congregation when they witnessed the massive fire-breathing monster force her way through the shattered window.

They began to panic and run, Father Josef leapt off the pew and tried to make it for the door, but Jade's powerful jaws clamped around his head and shook him violently. The bones in his neck snapped and he was hurled across the chapel.

People ran for the large church doors and tugged at them. Some tried to shove them open, anything to just escape the wrath of the dragon behind them. As soon as one man touched it, his hands burned from the fire on the other side.

Jade unleashed her fire breath, flames leapt from the podium and across pews. Villagers tried to run. One man picked up a chair and hurled it through a nearby window, but as he was climbing out, the dragon caught him by the legs and dragged him back in. His bones snapped and flesh ripped as Jade tore him apart with her claws.

***

Richard watched in stark horror from outside as the church became engulfed in flames. He saw the fires dancing through the windows both shattered and whole. He heard the terrified screams of the villagers trapped inside along with the vicious roars and growls of the dragon as it killed them.

The roof of the church began to crumble. Flames leapt out into the air as it collapsed in on itself. Smoke rose up into the sky and sparks burst out from the burning wood structure. Just then, the entire roof caved in. The church groaned and became unable to stand as explosion of flames erupted from the top. The walls collapsed in huge plumes of smoke. The terrified people inside fell silent.

All the strength drained from Richard's legs. He dropped the sword to the ground and fell to his knees. He watched as the remains of the church burned away, the crackle of the fire all around him was the only thing he heard. He broke down and sobbed.

Just when he thought it couldn't get any worse, a dragon's roar came from the burning skeleton of what used to be a church. He watched as a pair of wings emerge from the smoke and beat the smoke away. The dragon rose up into the air surrounded by fire and death.

The dragon lifted above the flames, their dancing flickering red light cast her in a devilish red glow. She roared, splitting the air. Richard could only watch in horror at this devil made flesh.

Amidst the crackling flames and the roaring dragon, Richard

missed another sound. The sound of a galloping horse. That is, until the horse came running right past him.

A man on horseback raced by at full gallop, his cape fluttered in the wind behind him. Richard blinked in astonishment as the horseman charged right up to the dragon. He held something in his hands, Richard soon recognized as a crossbow. Just as the rider approached the dragon, he fired a bolt which struck the beast in the chest.

Jade roared with anger at this new attacker. She breathed a stream of flames at him just as he turned the horse out of her range. The rider swiftly cocked the lever on the underside of the crossbow and fired again. The bolt struck the dragon in the left flank.

As Jade was about to prepare another attack, she caught a good look at the man on the horse. She noted his thick black hair, the beard which matched, and the crescent-shaped scar which covered half his face. She knew this human, she'd seen him before. This was the one who hunted her before, the man who forced her from her previous home.

Just as the rider locked his bow string in place and prepared to fire, Jade mustered her remaining strength. She took off with a powerful down stroke of her wings, leaving the village in burning rubble.

Chapter 23

Richard watched as the dragon flew away, its form becoming more and more distant until it was just a dark shape against the clouds. It was gone. Once again, he had failed. He punched at the ground and cried out in frustration and regret. "Grahhh!" His teeth clenched, tears leaked from his eyes.

A clopping of hooves alerted him to the approaching horseman. The rider climbed down from his mount. "Are you the lord responsible for this land?" He asked.

Richard wiped the tears from his face and stood. "I guess you could call me that. In truth, I was his squire, but he is dead now. So that leaves only me."

"A squire promoted to knight after his lord's death. I see." The man looked out at the burning village. He spotted Rachel laying in the snow. "We can discuss formalities later. First, you need to tend to that girl. And then work on containing this fire."

Richard gasped. "Rachel!" He ran to her side and fell in the snow beside her. "Rachel, please! Say something."

She groaned lightly as she shifted her head. She let out a gasp of pain when she tried to move her arm. Fresh blood seeped out of the gashes in her back.

"Oh, thank goodness. You're alive." Richard sobbed.

"She must be tended for immediately." The man said as he stepped up behind Richard, his crossbow slung over his shoulder. "Do you have a healer in this village?"

"We did, but I do not know if she is still alive or not." Richard responded.

The man nodded. "Take the girl there. Be careful when you carry her, she's already suffered enough."

Richard moved Rachel onto her back as gently as possible, still eliciting cried of agony from the girl as he did. It pained him each time he heard it, but he continued anyway. With her lying flat on her back, he slipped his arms under her leg and shoulders and carried her as swiftly and gingerly as he could to Helga's house.

As bad as the damage to some of the village was, not everything had been attacked by the dragon. He found Helga's home and most of that section to be still intact. After three strong knocks on the door, the large woman opened it. "Is it over?" She asked as she peered out. "I heard the devastation, how bad is it?"

"Pretty bad." Richard said. The smoke from the fires rose up to the sky behind him. "But right now, she needs your help." He motioned to Rachel in his arms.

"Oh, my goodness. Come on, bring her inside." Helga pulled the door all the way open. Richard followed her as she lead him to the secondary healing room with the straw mattress bed. He recognized it instantly as the room he was kept in. "Set her down on the bed. I'll prepare some hot water and set her wounds, but I'm afraid you can't stay."

"She stayed to help me." Richard protested. "Why can I not do the same for her?"

Helga hung a pot of water on the hook over her fireplace. "She is an unwed maiden. A man who is not her husband should not view her unclothed form. I can tend to her myself."

"But… she and I…" Richard began. He did not know how to explain his feelings, nor did he have the time.

Rachel stirred in the bed. She reached one arm up and placed it on Richard's cheek. She gave a tender smile before spoke. "We are wed,

Helga."

A look of shock came over Richard's face. He found himself unable to speak, but Helga's startle words said enough. "Wed?" The elder woman shouted. "How? When?"

"Before the dragon attacked." Rachel's voice was weak and strained, but she forced herself to continue. "We knew it was coming, and also knew we may not have time. So we asked Father Josef to marry us. We said the vows, spoke them from our hearts."

Richard's heart raced. He could hardly believe what he was hearing. He cupped Rachel's hand in his. His cheeks were wet with tears, he smiled with pure joy. These lies Rachel spoke were the most wonderful thing he'd heard in a long time. She wanted him to stay, and also wished to be his wife.

"Where is the good Father?" Helga demanded. "I must confirm this if it is true."

"Dead." Richard said. "Died in the church. The dragon killed him."

Helga threw her arms up in the air. "Well, isn't that just convenient! Fine! Stay if you wish, I don't care."

"He cannot." The crossbowman stepped into the room, his frame taking up much of the doorway. Everyone turned to look at him. "Squire, as I do not yet know your name, you are the current leader of this village. You must organize what survivors there are and work to douse the flames that still burn, or else you will have no village or newlywed wife."

Richard gave a look of sorrow. He knew this mercenary spoke the truth, but it pained him to have to leave Rachel's side, especially after everything she'd done for him. He planted a light kiss on her forehead. "I will return. I love you."

"As do I." She said.

"Yes, now please leave me to my work." Helga hurried him out the door and closed it behind him.

***

Vince watched as Richard departed. "Master Vince!" A voice called. He turned and saw his apprentice, Rennec, ride up to him with his horse and cart. "You saw it?"

"Yes, Rennec," he said as he faced the boy, "and it's the one. The one we've been tracking." He looked back over the devastation the dragon wrought upon this village. "Take the horses and stable them. I need to talk with this squire boy."

***

Once outside, Richard looked out over the burning village. In the sky above, clouds moved in and snow fell down upon the flames. It was a long process, but Richard found what few able bodied men he could and got them to work digging trenches around the burning structures. Taking the same shovels, they also threw snow from the ground upon the flames which hissed and popped as the frozen water smothered them. It was well after sunset when the fire was finally completely contained.

Richard led the survivors to *the Roaring Lion* tavern, the largest building which still stood. The bartender, Abel, set about getting as much food, drink, and blankets as he could for everyone.

He rested at the bar counter, his fingers pressed against his forehead. He sighed, exhausted. His whole body ached. A crossbow landed with a clunk on the counter next to and he jumped in startlement.

The man from before, the one with the scar over his face who scared off the dragon, propped himself against the counter, his arms folded over his chest. "What is you name, young man?" He asked.

Richard sat up straight, he held a fist to his mouth and cleared his throat. "Richard."

"Richard, then." The man said. "My name's Vince, dragon slayer. You say you were a squire. What happened to your lord?"

"It's a long story."

"We have time. If I'm to help you with this dragon problem, I need to know as much as I can." Vince said.

Richard scoffed. He rolled his eyes and looked over the small number of people in the tavern. “We’ve lost everything. Half of the village is ash, more than half of the people who lived here are dead. What can you do?”

“I can slay the dragon.” Vince replied. “I am a dragon slayer. I’ve been one most of my life, it’s what I do.” He motioned to the necklace adorned in stark white dragons teeth he wore. “This is my trophy display. Each one of these I took from a different dragon.”

“Well, congratulations.” Richard set his clenched fist on the bar counter. “You’ve bragged a little, now it’s my turn. This morning I set out with my lord, Sir Ardose, and a dragon slayer he hired named Cain to kill the beast.” Richard proceeded to tell the dragon slayer about Ardose’s plan to fleece the people of their gold and run away while the dragon burned them, how he was forced to kill the knight in self defense, how the townsfolk turned on him and beat him half to death before locking him in a closet, how they formed a mob and ascended the mountain only to unleash the fury of the dragon and get themselves killed as well as bring the monster back to the village and burn it to the ground.

Upon finishing his recount, Richard pounded his fist on the counter. “Abel!” He shouted. “Bring me an ale. I need a drink.” He took the pint when it was brought to him and drank half of it at once.

Vince gave a shrug. “Sounds like you had an eventful day.”

"I have." He took another swig of ale before setting the glass back down. "Now, tell me, what exactly do you know about dragons? You say you've hunted them most of your life, what have you learned form all that?"

"I've learned a few things." Vince spoke. "I know that females are larger and more dangerous than the males, especially when they have hatchlings. I'll tell you one thing: I've never seen a dragon do this before."

Richard looked up, he eyes the dragon slayer with confusion. "What do you mean? Don't dragons destroy things all the time? Towns and villages burned to the ground, virginal maidens sacrificed to placate the monster? Hoarding gold and riches?"

"Don't listen to mistrals. I know your recent experience my cloud your judgment, but dragons are just animals like any other. They care only about food, a cave to sleep in, and raising chicks." Vince said. "Now, they are not unintelligent, and they do not hunt humans for food. So I do not know why this one has chosen to attack you like this."

The door swung open and a young boy entered. He had curly red hair and a freckle dotted face. "Master Vince," he said, "I've stabled the horses and our supplies."

"Good work, Rennec." Vince pushed himself away from the counter. "We'll rest for the night and then set out in the morning." He turned back to Richard. “You said you’ve been to the dragon’s cave, yes?”

“I have.”

Vince gave a nod. “Good. Then you can lead me there in the morning.”

“You can guarantee that dragon will be dead?” Richard asked.

“I can.” Vince said. He took up his crossbow and stepped out of *the Roaring Lion.*

Chapter 24

Jade retreated to her mountain cave, the injuries in her ribs and flank stung in the cold air. Blood still oozed, but it had begun to clot now. Her flight back to the mountain had been laboriously long because of how much fire she used back at the village. Her internal supply of heat and flame was now almost extinguished, and would not be replenished anytime soon. She touched down outside the cave opening and walked inside.

That human, the one on the horse with that crossbow weapon, he was the one that attacked her in her previous home. What was he doing here? Had they tracked her all the way out here? She didn't care, she hated him just the same. She hated all humans.

She would return to the village and finish what she started. She would destroy the buildings, burn them to the ground and kill everyone who lived there. They would suffer for the death of her daughter, and the extermination and persecution of her race.

But her rampage would have to wait. She had used up much of her strength and her body was exhausted. She ached all over, and her hibernation was set to begin. Winter was upon her and the deep sleep beckoned.

Jade traveled deeper into the cave until she came upon the body of her daughter. The blood that once flowed though the hatchling's veins now lay in a frozen puddle on the ice. She pressed her snout against the hatchling's frost encrusted body, nuzzling it. This small display of affection was all she could give to her offspring now.

She laid down next to her daughter, her eyelids grew heavier than usual. Her breathing slowed to almost nothing as her heart rate dropped to only a few beats a minute. Her body entered into a state of suspended animation.

Jade would remain in this state for the next three and a half months, surviving off the energy reserves stored in her body. It would allow her to survive the winter, but it also shut off her internal heat source. And with it already depleted, she would neither be able to fly or breath fire upon awakening.

***

Richard approached Helga's house the next morning. Just as he came to the door, it swung open and the older, heavyset woman stepped outside. "Richard." she said, "Interesting you came by now. Come to visit your new bride?"

"I was, actually." He said. Her sudden appearance had startled him. "Where are you off to?"

"There are more people injured in this village than Rachel, and I'm the only person to tend to them." Helga said as she pulled her coat tighter around her body. "Sure, I might get some help from that bartender friend of yours, but aside from him I am on my own. You need not worry, Rachel is fine. She's recovering comfortably inside. Just don't visit for too long." Helga headed off for the tavern, leaving Richard behind.

He reached for the door, but stopped. He was anxious to see her, but how was he to approach Rachel now? Did she really want them to be wed? Did *he* really want that? He knew the answer, at least on his side, was yes. So, before he could stop himself again, he pushed the door open and stepped inside.

Richard found Rachel on the straw mattress in Helga's guest room. The large thick quilts were pulled up to her chin. She was wide awake, staring out the window by the bed with her fiery hair flung about across the pillow. She turned as soon as she heard the door open. Her face lit up when she saw Richard enter.

"You're back." She said, delighted. She pulled her arm out from under the blankets and held her hand out to him.

"Yes, I am." He crouched down on the floor beside the bed and rested his hands over hers. "But I'm not staying for too long. I'm setting out for the dragon's lair again today. I'm leading Vince and his apprentice to it."

Rachel tilted her head at the name. "Who's Vince?" She asked.

"Oh, that's right." Richard sheepishly said. He let out a small chuckle. "He's a dragon slayer with a substantial record, he's the one that drove it away yesterday."

"And you're going to take him to it?" Rachel's lower lip stuck out. "Must you?"

"I know where it is. I can take them to the cave and let them handle it from there." He said, running his fingertips over her arm. "It'll finally be over, Rachel. The dragon will die today, and then, if you would like, we can make our marriage official."

"Isn't it already? Helga believes us to be married."

"But no ceremony was performed. Father Josef never actually wed us." Richard stated. "I know you wished me to stay with you yesterday because you were afraid, but we are not truly man and wife."

“We could be.” With her one hand clasped in Richard’s palms, she peeked the fingers of her other hand above the quilt and slowly pushed it down. As the blanket slid past her shoulders, Richard saw they were bare. “All we need to do is consummate.”

He stared at the stunning pale skin as Rachel steadily slipped herself free of the smothering blankets. His face turned bright red. “Is that what you really want?” He asked as he turned away from her exposed skin to gaze into her emerald green eyes.

Her face was also flushed red. “Yes.” She answered in a quiet, almost whispered voice. Her heart raced, her whole body felt warmer than she’d ever known before.

Richard stood. He dropped her hand and walked back to the door. Rachel’s heart fell. She was sure he was about to leave her. Then he closed the door, set a chair propped up against it, and returned to her bedside. And in that moment, as he came back to her with a warm smile on his face, she never felt happier in her life.

***

Vince had been impatiently waiting by the edge of the village for over thirty minutes by the time Richard finally appeared. The young squire boy rode up on his horse with an almost stupid grin on his face. “You’re late.” Vince stated. He sat astride his own stallion and his apprentice, Rennec, rode next to him on a smaller, younger gelding. "I trust you had time to say your good-byes."

"I did." Richard said. "But I do intend to come back from this."

"As do I. Don't we always," Vince traced a finger along the crescent scar over his face. "But it is not a certainty. Did you bring a sword?"

"Yes," Richard patted the scabbard belted to his waist. It was one or Ardose's older swords, Lion's Fang had been taken by Phillip just before his own ill fated attempt at dragon slaying and was now, most likely, lost forever.

Vince gave a sharp nod. "Good." He had a sword as well, along with his crossbow. All three of them, Vince, Rennec, and Richard were dressed for battle, wearing their best armor and adorned with weapons. "Then, let us depart." He tugged on the reins of the horse and they rode off towards the mountain.

Chapter 25

Each step he took brought them closer to the cave. Vince rode up ahead of them, with Richard and Rennec riding a few yards behind. Richard moved his horse to walk right beside Rennec as he leaned over to talk. "You're his apprentice, right?"

"For a few years now, yes." Rennec replied. "Someday I hope to be a dragon slayer at least half as good as my master."

"Then maybe you can tell me something." Richard lowered his voice to a whisper. "That scar on his face, how did he get it?"

Rennec bit his lip. His eyes fell to his hands which gripped the reins. "He doesn't like to share that story. He'll point out the scar to people, but he doesn't often say how it came to be."

"But you know, right?"

Rennec nodded in response. "He's told me before. You cannot let him know I told you, understand?"

"Clearly." Richard said.

"Okay." Rennec took a deep breath, then let it out slowly. "When he was a child, Vince used to live on a farm with his family; his father, mother, and two brothers.

"When he was nine years old he heard a commotion out in the barn and went to investigate. Inside he found a dragon, a young male he would realize later, had killed one of the cows and was eating it.

"Vince was scared by the beast, as you could expect a nine-year-old to be. He screamed and it startled the dragon. It turned on him. He grabbed a nearby pitchfork to defend himself, but the dragon slashed at him and its claw caught his left cheek. It nearly took his whole face off.

"Young Master Vince cried out in pain, and this alerted his family back in the house. Their arrival frightened the dragon even more who then set everything on fire.

"The whole farm burned that night, all the animals died in the fire as they could not escape their stables. Vince had run out into the fields, and that action saved his life as the dragon attacked his family and killed them all. He looked back over the roaring fire to see the dragon taking off, and he swore vengeance against it.

"Now an orphan, Vince was forced to begging for food just to survive. That is until he met a traveling vagabond. This man, whose name I'm sure my master has mentioned before but I cannot remember, was a dragon slayer. He noted the injury to Vince's face, and after learning how he came to have it, decided to take the boy in and teach him the trade. Much later, Vince would enact his revenge on that very dragon that burned his family."

Richard listened with undivided vigor as Rennec concluded his story. He looked up at the mercenary ahead of him with a renewed sense of respect. "Last night at the tavern," he said, "Vince did not come off as having a deep resentment of dragons. Not like I would expect for a man of that history."

"That's because during his time hunting them, he's learned more." Rennec explained. "He knows that they are just animals that follow instinct the same as any other. They do not attack out of a malevolent desire to harm, usually they are just hungry or afraid."

"And what about what this one did to my village?"

Rennec gave a shrug. "I cannot say. I am still an apprentice. The best explanation I can give is that this is an anomaly, nothing more."

Vince held up his hand to single Richard and Rennec to stop. Ahead of them, scattered all about in the melted and then refrozen snow, lay corpses. Most were burnt, charred black. Others were covered in frost. Richard stared, open mouthed and shocked at the sight. “I take it this was your mob.” Vince stated as he climbed down from his horse.

“I… suppose so.” Richard also dismounted. He was horrified at the sight. Many of these people he had known and lived with his whole life.

Just above the scattered bodies, the mouth of a cave opened up from the face of the mountain. “And that,” Vince said with a point of his hand, “is the dragon’s cave?”

“Yes.” Richard replied.

“Good. Rennec!” Vince called to his apprentice. The young boy ran up to his master’s side as Vince handed the reins to him. “Tie off the horses someplace safe, then come right back.”

“Yes, sir.” Rennec said as he lead he horses away.

Vince slung he crossbow off his back and gripped it in both hands. He loaded the bottom compartment chamber with bolts. “Are you ready?” He motioned to Richard.

“Yes.” Richard drew his sword from the sheath.

“Good.” Vince said. “Rennec, torch, please.”

“Yes, sir.” Rennec stepped up in front of the dragon slayer with a wooden torch in his hand. He took one piece of flint and one of iron, struck them together, and set the end of the torch ablaze.

“Then let’s finish this.” Together, the three stepped into the cave.

***

Jade slept in the depths of her cave. All movement had ceased except for the very occasional rise and fall of her chest. Her hibernation had commenced, but her sleep was still light. The sounds of footsteps and the smell of burning wood awoke her from hibernation. She knew what was here. The humans had come for her again. And the scent of one was most familiar, she recognized it as the same one that had attacked her so many times before. She loathed him the most.

Her lips curled and she snarled. A deep, rumbling hiss from her throat that escaped through her needle-sharp teeth. Jade stood and shook out the stiffness in her muscles. Then, with very deliberate movements, she advanced towards the human invaders.

She would not run again, she was tired of running, tired of hiding. Now, she was going to stand her ground and fight for her right to live. This was to be the last stand of the dragon.

Chapter 26

Richard, Vince, and Rennec crept through the dark cavernous halls of the rocky cave. The light from Rennec's torch danced and flickered with the flames. A sense of déjà vu seeped into Richard's mind. Only yesterday he walked along these same steps hunting the same dragon. It just happened to be with a different dragon slayer. His heart raced, his eyes moved furiously around in their sockets as he glanced from one moving shadow to the next. Somewhere in this cave lurked Jade, the dragon.

He placed one hand on his chest, closed his eyes, and took a deep breath to steady himself. He inhaled through his nose and back out through his mouth.

"You feel alright?" Vince asked in a hushed voice.

"Just a little anxious." He took back up his sword.

A deafening roar bellowed from the depths of the cave. All three of them froze in their tracks, they stared down into the long shadows and eternal darkness. None of them moved, they barely breathed.

The sound of disturbed stones was heard. A soft padding of feet along with the hard clink of claws as something approached. She emerged from the darkness like a thief in the night; her shoulders hunched, claws extended, wings folded, lips curled, and teeth bared.

Almost nine feet tall, twenty-five feet long, and over a ton of deadly, angry reptile advanced like a large cat stalking its prey. The shadows dripped off her as she walked into the torch light like globes of black ink. She was Jade the dragon.

Richard lifted his sword. He gripped the pommel with both hands. "I've waited too long for this day."

"Be on your guard." Vince stated. "This is its territory, we don't know what to predict." He raised the crossbow and aimed. With a tug of the trigger, the bowstring snapped forward.

The bolt propelled towards the dragon and grazed the side of her face. Jade hissed, fresh blood oozed down form the small cut.

"Why did you miss?" Richard asked.

"Because I did. It's dark and the light is not good. Not every shot can be perfect." Vince said as he cocked the lever and the crossbow reloaded. The dragon drew in a deep breath. "She's preparing to breathe fire. Richard, I suggest you go back outside."

"I'm not leaving, this is my mission, too." Richard protested.

"No time to argue. You don't have a flame cloak, go outside!" Vince grabbed him roughly and pushed him back towards the cave entrance. "Once we've forced her to burn away all her fire, we'll call you back in!"

Richard began to see the plan. He gave a quick nod and raced back to the sunlight.

Jade's gaze was drawn to the movement. She watched the human, Richard, as he sheathed his sword and ran away from her. She would not let any human escape her cave now, least of all him. She roared in anger and chased after him.

"Hey!" Vince shouted. He fired the crossbow, and this time the bolt struck the dragon in the gut. She growled with pain. "You want a fight, come at me!" Vince pumped the lever and fired bolt after bolt, they rained down on the dragon. She snarled and growled, shook her head from side to side as the bombardment continued. Vince's chamber was soon out. He crouched down and grabbed hold of his clock, holding it up in front of himself like a shield. "Rennec, get down!"

Jade drew back her head and unleashed all the fire she could muster. Only small, blue flames escaped past her tongue. She tried again, but nothing happened. Her internal heat was gone from hibernation; her fire was out.

She didn't care now. She bellowed an earsplitting roar, her muscles tensed, and she charged her invaders. Rennec peeked out from behind his cloak only to see the rapidly approaching dragon. He shrieked, dropped his cloak, and tried to run, but the dragon was too close. Jade overtook him, her jaws clamped tightly over his shoulder and bones crunched beneath her teeth.

She shoved past Vince, knocking him to the ground. He cried out in surprise as he landed hard on his back, wincing in pain. He heard the snarls and growls, the screaming and snapping of bone. In shook and horror, he witness the dragon shake Rennec like a dog. Her teeth easily shred the light armor he wore and tore through the young boy's skin and flesh. Rennec cried in agony, unable to free himself or even utter any coherent words, only shrieks of pain.

Jade tossed the boy aside and there was a sickening crunch as his skull cracked against the rock wall. His screams stopped instantly.

"Rennec!" Vince shouted. He stood up and took his crossbow again, fitted it with another chamber of bolts, and began to fire. "You want to do it like that, huh? Well, come on then!" Vince's voice shook as he spoke.

Jade winced and backed away as the bolts stuck in her scales. Her throat rumbled with anger. Once the bolts stopped and Vince moved to reload, Jade attacked. She pounced on him, knocking the crossbow from his hands. She pinned him down, her clawed foot pressed him against the ground and her talons pierced the armor breastplate.

Vince gasped under the weight of the dragon. He struggled, pulled a dagger from his belt and stabbed it deep in the dragon's leg. Jade roared, pulled her leg back and limped in pain. Blood spilt down her foot and dripped from her claws. She yanked the knife out with her jaws, scarlet blood splattered across the cave walls.

Taking his sword from the scabbard, Vince jumped to his feet and moved to attack. He'd fought dragons before, often with just a sword, but none like this. This beast was vicious and ruthless, she seemed not to care for her own safety, but more about killing her targets.

Jade lunged at Vince, her mouth agape and teeth bared. She reached out with her front claws. Just before she caught him, Vince threw himself at the ground. He ducked and rolled under the dragon, her claws embedded in the stone cave wall. He righted himself and brought his sword to bare. He was about to thrust it into the dragon's gut when Jade kicked her hind leg out and struck him, sending Vince skidding across the ground. The sword slipped from his hands.

Vince gasped for air. Jade knocked the wind out of him with that last kick. His body trembled as he sat up. A loud crash split the air as Jade broke free of the rocks. She turned towards the human, rage and hate in her eyes. For the first time since his childhood, Vince found himself absolutely terrified of a dragon.

He looked around frantically for his sword. It slipped from his hands after the dragon kicked him, leaving him unarmed. He found it behind him, closer to the cave entrance. If he ran, he could get it and fight back before the dragon caught him, but he would have to be fast.

Vince bolted to his feet and sprinted for the exit, the dragon roared as it gave chase. He was fast, Jade was faster. The dragon pounced and pinned him to the ground, his face pressed up against the rough stone.

The claws dug into his back, the dragon's weight crushed him. But it was so close now. Vince reached out with his good hand for the sword, his fingertips almost touched the end of the hilt. If he could just reach a little more then he might…

Jade clamped her jaws around Vince's head. Her three inch teeth pierced his skull. He knew it was coming, even if he could grab the sword it would do nothing for him now. It was over. Jade jerked her head sharply to the side, Vince's head ripped from his neck in a fountain of blood.

The dragon dropped the human's severed head to the ground where it landed with a wet splat. Two of them were now dead, that left only the one outside. The one who caused her all this pain.

Richard waited, anticipated, out in the snow. His back was pressed against a tree and he faced away from the cave. He dared not to look inside as he heard the cries of terror and death. The first death he knew was Rennec, the poor boy whose dream was to be a dragon slayer like Vince, only to be killed by one instead. Then there was a struggle, and finally a sickening snap and crunch, but he didn't know who or what caused it.

Finally, curiosity overruled his better judgment and he peered around the tree to look. At first, he caught just its dark shape hidden in the shadow, and then it emerged into the light and he saw it. Jade, the dragon, with bolts from Vince's crossbow sticking out of her scales like quills and blood coating her muzzle.

Jade stood at the edge of her cave, she growled and snarled. A brief instant of movement caught her eye, the other human. He stood behind a tree less than thirty feet from her. She roared, blood and saliva flew from her fangs, and charged for him.

Richard bolted away from the oncoming monster. He ran from the tree and headed deeper into the woods. A loud splintering of wood could be heard as the tree he'd just ran from came crashing down, Jade having torn through its trunk.

She pursued him, while unable to fly she could use her wings to gain speed as she stalked her prey. Richard could hardly keep out of her reach, more than once as he veered out of her path he caught the wind of her claws or of her snapping teeth. Fear drove him to run. Fear and adrenaline. The same dragon he had so foolishly tried to attack in a field was now chasing him like a fox after a rabbit.

His foot caught on a root buried in the snow and he plunged face first to the ground. Jade was upon him in less than a second. Before she could tear his head off the same as Vince, Richard tore Ardose's old sword from its sheath and struck the dragon across the face. Jade winced and retreated in surprise, the blade sliced through her scales and drew another swath of blood. He got back to his feet, but rather than flee again, he took the sword and stared down the dragon.

Jade lunged at him, snapping her jaws and swiping her talons, but Richard held her back. He swung at her again, and Jade pulled back.

He was doing it. He was fighting the dragon, and somehow he was keeping it at bay. He could do it, he could do what everyone else failed to. He could slay the dragon. Richard pulled back the sword and thrust it at her head. Jade clamped her powerful jaws over the steel blade and twisted, the sword shattered. Shards of metal fell to the snow and dribbled out from her teeth.

Richard stared, dumbstruck at the stump of a sword he now held. His one good defense, the only weapon he had, the dragon snapped it into pieces without a seconds thought. Without thinking, he hurled the broken hilt at Jade and ran as fast as he could.

The pommel struck Jade in the face. She winced as the guard hit her eye and then bounced harmlessly away. She roared and gave chase again. She would not let him get away, not this time.

Richard's legs ached as he ran. The dragon was right behind him, and there was no where left for him to go. In another moment she would be on top of him, her claws in his chest and her teeth at his neck. Out of the corner of his eye he saw something in the snow. Something that glittered like gold. With the dragon ready to lunge, Richard scooped it up and looked down at it stupidly. It was Lion's Fang! His sword, the one Phillip stole the day before! And it was said to be sharp enough to cut dragon scales. Now he could do it. Now, he could slay the dragon.

Richard came to a halt just before he turned back to face the dragon. He gripped the sword in both hands and let out a battle cry as he charged. Jade pounced at her prey, her mouth wide open and all her needle sharp teeth prepared to render flesh. They collided, Richard stabbed the sword forward just as Jade snapped her jaws shut.

Bones buckled and broke under the pressure of her jaws. Richard's punctured lungs filled with his own blood as Jade's teeth pushed deeper into them, punctured his skull, and closed around his face like a prison cage. His vision grew blurry. His blood soaked hands were too weak to hold on anymore and they slipped from the sword, falling to his side.

He coughed and convulsed in the dragon's mouth, blood splattered down his chin. This was the end, and he knew it. His eyes rolled back into his head as they closed and his heart stuttered to a stop. The last thought to go through his dying mind was that of Rachel; asleep, warm, and happy in the bed waiting for his return. Then, he breathed his last breath and his life lifted from his body.

Jade dropped Richard's lifeless body to the ground. His corpse landed with a thump against the snow at her feet. He was dead. The ones who had plagued her existence ever since she came to this mountain were finally gone, the last one now lay dead at her feet.

A sudden convulsion pulsed through her body. She gagged, blood came spewing from her mouth; not human blood. Her legs felt weak, her whole body was wracked with spasms of pain. The long steel blade of Richard's sword, Lion's Fang, pierced straight through her chest and stabbed her heart.

Jade's legs gave out beneath her. She collapsed to the ground, her body landed on Richard's. She tried to stand, but all her energy had been drained. The dragon did not even have the strength to return to her cave and die with her daughter. Her blood mingled with that of her enemy, her eyes grew dim. Jade stopped struggling, instead she fell to the earth and let death take her. Her eyes closed and her pierced heat beat its last.

The last dragon died.

Chapter 27

Rachel lay soundly in the spare bed of Helga's house. Her face was buried in the pillow, her hair a wild mess, blankets strewn over her body. She lay in a half sleep state, her eyes closed and a small smile upon her lips. Her dreams were of Richard, she longed for his return. Her rest was disturbed when a knock came to the door. "Rachel?" Helga's voice called from the other side. "Are you decent? My I enter?"

"Helga?" Rachel's voice was groggy. "What is it?"

Helga pushed the door open, she drug her rocking chair in with her and took a seat in the corner. Rachel sat up in bed, the blanket pulled up to her collarbone to cover her otherwise exposed self. "What's going on?" She asked as she saw the sadness and stark whiteness of Helga's face. "What happened? Does it have to do with Richard?"

The older woman took a handkerchief from her sleeve and rubbed the tears from her eyes. "Richard came to visit you this morning, I'm sure you're aware, just before he set out with the dragon slayers."

"Yes." Rachel replied, although she did not confess to what she and he did just before his leaving. "Had he returned?"

"Their horses, all three of them, came charging back into the village just this past hour." Helga spoke. "All were close to death from exhaustion having run themselves so hard, and all were without their rider."

Rachel felt her heart stop with shock, her blood ran cold and the color drained from her face. "No…" She whispered almost too quiet for even herself to hear. "I don't believe you. He can't be…"

"I'm sorry I had to be the one to tell you." Helga stood and approached the redhead. She placed a hand on Rachel's shoulder, only for it to be swatted away.

"No!" Rachel spat. "He's coming back! He has to! I don't believe that he'd be…" She looked up at Helga with tears streaming down her face and her teeth clenched. "All we know is that his horse came back. Maybe it just got frightened off and now he's walking down the mountain! Has anyone thought of that?!"

"We have considered it, but it's not likely. Rachel," Helga sat on the bed next to the younger woman. This time, the girl did not bat her away. "You must accept it. He's not coming back. His mission was a failure."

She was unable to hold back her tears any longer. Rachel wept, her face buried in the blankets as she cried with grief and misery. The fabric quickly soaked through. "I will not accept it!" She wailed. "I need to see for myself!"

"That's not possible. This time of year, no one should venture up that mountain." Helga said. "And besides, it's too late in the day. The sun is almost set already, it would be pure darkness by the time you even reached anything close to the dragon's lair."

"Fine then, first thing tomorrow." Rachel groaned. "But I will make sure, even if I have to go alone."

* * *

Rachel had a horse saddled and ready to ride that next morning. She sat astride it, one leg on each side rather than sidesaddle. She kept a dagger in its scabbard at her waist, unwilling to travel up this mountain unarmed.

But she was alone. No one else from the village dared to go with her, all of them were too frightened of the thought that the dragon might still be alive.

She pushed the horse further up the mountain slopes, it huffed and puffed for breath. Thick clouds of whitish vapor formed around the animal's muzzle. Rachel followed the tracks left in the snow from the days before; she was no expert in detecting animal tracks by any means, but the footprints left by both Phillip's mob and later Richard's venture were easy to find.

Soon, she came upon the devastation that surrounded the mouth of the dragon's cave. The frost covered, burnt bodies of Phillip's mob lay in scattered remains in the snow. She placed her hand over her mouth in shock and horror. Looking from the charred corpses to the yawning maw of the cave, she feared to enter.

From a distance came the caw of a crow. She tugged the reins of the horse and lead it towards the sound. In a small clearing in the woods, she found the black bird and what it was pecking at. Rachel gasped.

Richard's body lay face down in the snow, which was now red with his blood. On top of him lay the dragon, enormous and frightening even in death. Both the man and dragon were encrusted in ice. "Richard!" She shouted so loud it scared the crow away.

Rachel leapt off the horse and ran to Richard's side. It took all her strength, but she managed to drag him free from the dragon's clutched, his body was riddled with teeth marks. "No, no. Not you. Can't be dead." She held his cold form in her arms, buried her face in his chest, and sobbed. She'd hoped against all reason to find him alive, but now her searching was in vain. Richard had been slain just the same as all the others.

She placed a kiss upon his forehead. He was cold to the touch, and that coldness pierced her soul. She couldn't just leave him here, he deserved better than that. Richard deserved a proper burial.

Rachel laid him on his back, and after looking about for a moment spotted the wooden handle of a shovel, one of the tools brought by Phillip's mob two days prior. Rachel took it, and still fighting through her tears, she got to work. She first cleared away a section of snow the length of Richard's body, and then stabbed the shovel at the ground. The earth was cold, hard, and unyielding. The day wore on and shadows grew long as she dug the makeshift grave. Her hands ached with blisters, droplets of sweat froze on her forehead. Finally, with the sun already slipping behind the mighty jagged peaks of the mountains, she tossed the shovel aside with the hole dug.

With what strength she still had, Rachel placed Richard's body in the shallow grave. She crossed his arms over his chest and closed his eyes. Aside from the wounds and the paleness of his skin, he looked almost peaceful, like he was just sleeping and would awaken at any moment. This thought only brought more tears to Rachel's eyes. Blinking them away, she got to work filling in the grave.

Once she was done, Rachel tossed the shovel aside. An elevated mound of dirt lay at her feet. She was exhausted, her whole body ached, but she still had to do one last thing. Glittering in the dying sunlight, she saw the hilt of Richard's sword, Lion's Fang, still embedded in the dragon’s chest. Rachel grasped it with both hands and pulled with every ounce of strength she could muster. Slowly, the blade slipped away from the dragon’s corpse. Once freed, she brought it back to Richard’s burial mound and stabbed it into the ground as a grave marker.

Rachel mounted her horse again, dried her tears on her sleeve, and with a kick, signaled her horse back down the mountain. She stole a glance over her shoulder at the grave of the man she loved.

Her return to the village somehow seemed shorter than the journey to the mountain cave. She wished it hadn't, she wanted more time alone with her thoughts and emotions before coming back. Helga was there to greet her just as Rachel rode into the village.

“You're back, and you're safe. I'm grateful.” The elder woman said as she took the reins. Rachel didn't give a response. She solemnly stared at the ground and slowly lifted herself off the horse. “What is it?”

“You were right.” Rachel said, quietly. “He's dead.” Tears began to flow fiercely now, streaming down her face like miniature waterfalls. “I wanted... I wished... ” she said between her crying gasps for air, “that he might have lived. That we could live together.”

Helga took her handkerchief and dabbed it on Rachel's face. Even as the tears dried, new ones took their place. “But you found him, right? And you found the dragon?”

Rachel's lip quivered as she forced her tears back. She gave a swift nod. “Yes. He killed it, they killed each other.”

“Then he died to save us. To save you and everyone in this village.” Helga reassured her. “He died like a knight.”

Rachel took a deep breath. Her tears were drying now, and hearing Helga's words helped to clear her mind. “Yes, he was our knight.”

www.ingramcontent.com/pod-product-compliance
Lightning Source LLC
Chambersburg PA
CBHW030816310726
48980CB00006B/510/J
9781947583047